OUTLAW RANGER #5

GUN DEVILS OF THE RIO GRANDE

James Reasoner

Outlaw Ranger #5: Gun Devils of the Rio Grande by James Reasoner

Cover Design Livia Reasoner

ISBN-13: 978-1532826375
ISBN-10: 1532826370
Rough Edges Press
www.roughedgespress.com
Rough Edges Press

Table of Contents

Chapter 1

Hell came to Santa Rosalia while the village slept. The raiders charged in on horseback, shouting and shooting, when the eastern sky had barely begun to show streaks of red and gold. Men hurried out of their jacals to see what was going on and were shot down, swiftly and brutally. Their bullet-riddled bodies flopped in the dust and their women ran to them, falling to their knees, weeping and wailing.

The screams grew louder as the raiders dismounted and jerked the women away from their slain loved ones—but only the women young and pretty enough. Then the killers strode into the *jacals* to search for more women and girls. They kicked aside the boys who put up a fight. The old women who tried to protect their daughters and granddaughters and nieces were gunned down just as the village's men had been.

In the end, the only ones left living in Santa Rosalia were the very young, the very old, the infirm, and the women so ugly no man would ever want them. And since most women grew beautiful when a man guzzled down enough tequila, there were very few of those.

The raiders found a number of carts in the village, normally used in the farming that gave these people their livelihood. They forced the prisoners into those carts, where they huddled together in their nightclothes, stunned and terrified. Then the men brought donkeys from their pens and hitched them to the carts. The crude vehicles lurched into motion and rolled northwest from Santa Rosalia, following the course of the river that divided Mexico from Texas.

Some of the weeping women looked across the river at the level, brush-dotted terrain. The *Tejanos*, many of them anyway, were regarded as devils who liked nothing better than to kill

Mexicans. But right now, these prisoners would have welcomed the sight of a band of bloody-handed Texans charging across the Rio Grande to kill their captors.

No help waited for them, in Texas or elsewhere. The carts rolled slowly past several men who sat on their horses in the growing light and studied the prisoners. Martin Larrizo's mount stood slightly ahead of the other two. His lieutenants flanked him. He nodded slowly, satisfied with what he saw.

He lifted a hand and pointed at one of the young women. "That one."

Hector Gonsalvo spurred forward and leaned down toward the prisoners. The women cringed from him but couldn't get away. Gonsalvo looped a long, ape-like arm around the captive Larrizo had pointed out and dragged her from the cart as she screamed and punched futilely at him. He rode with her back toward Larrizo, then reined in and dropped her on the ground next to his horse.

He held on tight to her nightdress, though, so it ripped away from her as she fell, leaving her slender body nude. She hunkered on the ground, doubling over in an attempt to hide her nakedness.

Larrizo, tall in the saddle, barrel-chested, with a heavy-jawed face and thick mustache, nodded to Gonsalvo. The lieutenant dismounted, wrapped sausage-like fingers in the girl's long black hair, and jerked her to her feet, putting her body on blatant display. Larrizo nodded.

"This one is mine," he said. "No one touches her." He lifted his voice and addressed all his men. "No one touches *any* of them until we know what value they are to us." He looked at Gonsalvo again. "Bring her, Hector."

Gonsalvo lifted the young woman, who struggled for a second before going limp, as if all her resistance, all her hope, had run out of her like water. He placed her on Larrizo's horse in front of the leader, who looped his left arm around her waist and jerked the reins with his right hand to turn the big black horse. The rowels of his spurs raked the animal's flanks and it leaped forward into a gallop.

Martin Larrizo rode like the wind away from the conquered

village with his prize firmly in his grasp.

But this was just the beginning, and a much greater prize waited out there for him to seize it.

All of Mexico.

Chapter 2

Braddock sat in the opulent bar of the Camino Real Hotel in El Paso and nursed a beer. His surroundings—gleaming hardwood, polished brass, sparkling crystal—were a far cry from what he was accustomed to in his simple adobe cabin in Esperanza, the Mexican village downriver that had become his home.

The Camino Real boasted all sorts of guests. Mexican *grandees* and *hacendados*, Texas cattlemen, railroad tycoons, successful businessmen of all stripes...and their ladies, gowned and coiffed and perfumed, possessed of all the loveliness money could buy. It wasn't exactly the sort of place where a disgraced former lawman would spend an evening. A man wanted by the authorities on this side of the river.

An outlaw Ranger.

Braddock was tall, lean, deeply tanned, with a scar running up the side of his face into his sandy hair. He wore a brown suit that was nothing fancy, especially compared to the garb of the bar's other patrons but still the best outfit he owned. A cream-colored Stetson with a tightly curled brim sat on the table.

Most folks didn't parade around with guns on their hips anymore, not in the early days of this new, modern century, so Braddock had left his shell belt and Colt at the boarding house where he had rented a room. He had an over/under .41 caliber derringer tucked in his waistband just above the watch pocket where he carried the badge he had once worn as a member of the Texas Rangers, the West's most famous outlaw hunters.

He might not have a legal right to that vaunted emblem anymore, but it never left his possession. A bullet had punched a hole right in the center of the badge.

He took another sip of the beer and looked around the room,

studying the faces of the people without being too obvious about it. He had come here to meet someone, but he didn't know the man by sight.

A letter for Braddock had made its way to Esperanza, where mail delivery was an uncertain thing to begin with. It was no real secret Braddock lived in the village, but he didn't think too many people north of the border knew about it.

A man named E.J. Caldwell had sent the letter, which asked that Braddock meet him at the Camino Real in El Paso to discuss a business arrangement. Also inside the envelope, Braddock found a fifty dollar greenback.

Braddock could have stuck the bill in his pocket, thrown away the letter, and forgotten the whole thing. It would have been easy enough to do, and he'd considered it.

But his friend the padre, who was there when Braddock read the letter, had smiled and said, "You are curious, my friend. You want to know who this man is, how he knows about you...and what he wants you to do."

"Curiosity's not a sin, is it?"

"No. But it can be a temptation that *leads* one into sin."

"You can't know where a trail goes unless you follow it," Braddock had said, and the next morning he had gathered a few supplies, saddled his dun horse, and ridden toward El Paso after telling the priest goodbye and adding, "I'll be back."

"I pray to *El Señor Dios* it is so."

Braddock left the fifty bucks with the padre. If he didn't come back, the money might as well stay where it could do some good. Braddock had only a few needs: food, shelter, ammunition.

He couldn't afford to stay at the Camino Real, so he found more suitable accommodations. Then he'd shaken out his suit, brushed his hat, stuck the derringer in his waistband, and come here to meet Mr. E.J. Caldwell.

Who might just be the stocky, florid-faced gent with curling mustaches coming toward Braddock now. He looked like the sort of man who could stick a fifty dollar bill in an envelope without thinking twice about it.

He had a drink in one hand and a derby in the other. Braddock kept an eye on the derby, which might have a gun hidden in it, although such a crude subterfuge in a room as fancy as this seemed out of place. The man stopped on the other side of the table and said, “Mr. Braddock? G.W. Braddock?”

“Who’s asking the question?”

“E.J. Caldwell, sir. Would you object if I sat down?”

“That depends. How much did you pay for this meeting?”

The man smiled and said, “Ah, testing my bona fides. The amount in question is fifty simoleons, my friend.”

Braddock didn’t like it when people he didn’t know took him for their friend, but he let it pass. He gestured with his left hand for Caldwell to sit down. His right hand lay easily in his lap, handy to the derringer.

Caldwell set the glass of whiskey and the derby on the table and took a seat. “I’m very happy you saw fit to meet me,” he said. “I didn’t know exactly when you’d arrive, so I’ve been checking here every evening for a week.”

“You knew what I look like?”

“I had an excellent description of you.”

And where had he gotten that description, Braddock wondered. Off a reward poster? He knew charges had been levied against him, and the Rangers, at least some of them, would like to see him in custody, but he didn’t know if they had circulated posters on him. He could have asked Caldwell and pressed for an answer, he supposed, but he wasn’t sure it was worth the trouble just yet.

Instead he asked, “What can I do for you, Mr. Caldwell?”

“First of all, you should understand the fifty dollars was to pay for your time and trouble coming up here.”

Braddock smiled faintly. “That’s sort of what I figured.”

“I have a business proposition for you, and if you take the job, there’ll be further remuneration. A goodly amount, in fact.”

“How goodly?”

Caldwell put out a fat-fingered hand and wobbled it a little. “That’s a matter for negotiation.”

Something bristled inside Braddock. He wasn’t a hired gun. He had been a lawman, and when he’d lost his badge not through any fault of his own but through corrupt political shenanigans, he had continued bringing owlhoots to justice, even though that put him on the wrong side of the law as far as some were concerned.

The idea of sitting here and haggling with this man put a bitter taste in his mouth. Had he really come to this? To hell with it. He didn't even care what the job was anymore. He drank the rest of the beer and set the empty glass on the table between them.

"Forget it."

Caldwell's bushy eyebrows rose in surprise. "Excuse me?"

"I said forget it. I don't want the job. I don't care what it pays. I'm not a hired gun."

"Please, Mr. Braddock, don't be hasty. Perhaps I didn't make it clear how urgent this matter is."

"It's not urgent to me," Braddock said. He scraped his chair back and started to stand up.

"I've offended you. That wasn't my intention. I know you're not a gunman for hire. You're a Texas Ranger."

That made Braddock pause and settle back in his chair. His history wasn't that hard to look up. There had even been a few newspaper stories written about him, although he wasn't what anybody would call a notorious character.

Caldwell leaned forward and went on, "It really is vital that I talk to you and explain the whole situation, but not here."

That raised Braddock's hackles. "Where, then?"

"I have a room upstairs."

Well, that had *trap* written all over it. Could Caldwell be working for Captain Hughes? If he went up to the man's room, would he find it full of Rangers waiting to clap him in irons and haul him off to jail? The Rangers had gone to elaborate lengths to catch outlaws in the past. He wasn't sure they actually wanted him that badly, but on the other hand he sort of gave the organization a bad name by tackling problems they couldn't take on in their currently hamstrung operation.

Anyway, there was that curiosity again, the temptation the padre had warned him about.

On still one more hand, Braddock was pretty sure he was going to hell no matter what he did, so why not give in? It might just get him there quicker.

"All right," he said, reaching for his hat. "Let's go."

Caldwell looked a little surprised again, as if he hadn't really expected Braddock to agree this quickly. But he picked up his derby—turning it so Braddock could see no gun was hidden in it, although Braddock figured such a revelation wasn't the man's intention—and said, "Thank you. I appreciate you indulging me."

The Camino Real had an elevator, the first in this whole part of the country. Braddock didn't like it much as the little cage rattled and shook and lifted them to the hotel's third floor. Like most things about an increasingly modern world, it just didn't seem right to him. He didn't show that on his face, though, as he rode up with Caldwell.

"My suite is right down here," the man said as they walked along a hallway with a thick carpet runner on the floor. Gilt wallpaper covered the corridor's walls, and fancy sconces held gas lamps that hissed faintly.

Caldwell paused in front of a door and took a key out of his pocket. He unlocked it, turned the knob, pushed the door open an inch or so, glanced over his shoulder to smile at Braddock.

Braddock planted his left hand in the middle of Caldwell's back and shoved hard. As Caldwell exclaimed in alarm and crashed into the door, Braddock palmed out the derringer. Caldwell stumbled across the room, lost his balance, and planted himself face first. Luckily for him he landed on a well-upholstered divan. He rolled off it and half-sat, half-lay in the floor looking stunned. His derby had fallen off.

Braddock didn't see anybody else, but somewhere in the room a woman laughed and said, "Such a dramatic entrance wasn't really necessary, Mr. Braddock, but please, come in."

Chapter 3

Braddock's hand tightened on the derringer. He had expected he might find trouble up here, but not a woman.

Of course, those two things often went together.

When he didn't move, the unseen woman went on, "This isn't a trap, I assure you, although I admit, I did get you up here on false pretenses. A little anyway."

The man sitting on the floor had recovered enough from his surprise to flush with anger. He looked to his left, glared, and said, "You didn't pay me enough to be manhandled like that, lady. I don't care how pretty you are."

That was intriguing. Braddock hadn't been with a woman in quite a while, but he was no more immune to their charms than any other man. The comment just added to his curiosity.

A twenty dollar gold piece sailed toward the man, bounced off his chest, and landed on the floor beside him. The man still glared, but he picked up the coin.

"There's a bonus," the woman said. "You can get out now, since you've outlived your usefulness. I should have known it was better just to be honest and forthright."

The man scrambled to his feet, made some huffing noises, and left the room, stepping quickly to the side as soon as he came through the door so he could give Braddock a wide berth. He stomped off down the hall, glancing back in a mixture of anger and nervousness, as if worried Braddock might come after him.

For the most part, Braddock had already forgotten about the man. He focused his attention on the woman inside the room, who said without moving into view, "Well? Are you coming in or not?"

Braddock stepped across the threshold and swung to his right, toeing the door back farther so he could see the woman.

He pointed the derringer at her. She didn't flinch.

She looked like she didn't flinch from much. She leveled cool and intelligent blue eyes at him. Blond hair put up in a stylish bun topped an attractive face. The dark blue dress the woman wore hugged the appealing curves of her body.

"You'd be Miss E.J. Caldwell, I reckon," Braddock said.

"Elizabeth Jane Caldwell, yes. I use the initials professionally."

"What sort of *profession* are we talking about that requires a woman to use her initials?"

She frowned and said, "Don't be crude, Mr. Braddock. It doesn't become you." She gestured toward a silver tray with a pot and a couple of china cups on it. "Coffee? Of course, you'd have to put up that gun in order to drink it."

"If you'll pour, I can manage one-handed, thanks."

She burst out in a laugh. "Oh, come on. Surely you don't think I'm that much of a threat. What am I going to do, bushwhack you?" She moved her hands to indicate her body. "I'm not exactly toting a six-shooter."

"Yeah, well, a fella never knows. But the way you throw money around, I suppose you've earned a little indulgence."

He slipped the derringer back inside his waistband.

"Thank you," she said. "I've had guns pointed at me before. It's never a pleasant experience."

"I could say the same thing. Only the ones pointed at me usually go off."

"I've had that happen, too," she said as she poured coffee in the china cups.

"Is that so? You don't look like the sort of lady who winds up in gunfights."

"I wind up all sorts of places you wouldn't expect me to be."

She handed Braddock one of the cups. He sipped the coffee, found it to be as good as you'd expect in a place like the Camino Real. He said, "This drawing room banter is amusing as all hell, but I'd just as soon get down to business."

"I agree. Have a seat. Take off your hat."

Braddock looked around. The room had a couple of plushly upholstered wing chairs in it, to go along with the divan. All of them would be difficult to get up from in a hurry if a man needed to. A straight-backed wooden chair sat at a writing desk. He picked it up, swung it around, and straddled it. He put his hat on the floor beside him.

"Are you always this careful?" Elizabeth Jane Caldwell asked as she sat on the divan.

"Generally."

"I suppose a man in your position has to be."

"My position?"

"A man with a lot of enemies...on both sides of the law."

She drew her legs up partially underneath her. Braddock couldn't tell if it was a calculated move or if she was just getting comfortable, but he thought it made her look like a magazine illustration. One of those, what were they called, Gibson girls, that was it.

"Look, Miss Caldwell, you don't have to try to charm me. You got me here for a business deal. I reckon you hired that fella to pretend to be you because you thought if you showed up downstairs, I wouldn't talk to you."

"Yes, that's what I meant about false pretenses. That man is a salesman. Smith, Johnson, some sort of plain name, I don't know, but I met him here in the hotel and thought he might prove useful. If I've offended you, I apologize."

Braddock shrugged. "I'm not offended. It just wasn't necessary. I don't care if you're a man or a woman. Your money spends the same either way."

"Well, it's not exactly *my* money..."

"It comes from the newspaper you write for, doesn't it?"

"So you know who I am. You probably knew all along, didn't you?"

Braddock didn't say anything. To tell the truth, it had just come to him. When he'd seen the name E.J. Caldwell on the letter, it hadn't meant a damn thing to him. But he supposed a memory had been lurking in the back of his head, and it had chosen this moment to come forward.

"I've seen the name on stories you've written. Didn't know you were a lady. You don't write like a woman—and I don't mean just your hand on that letter you sent me."

"They're just words on paper, Mr. Braddock," she said with a faint sharp edge to her voice. "They don't know whether it's a man or a woman writing them."

"I suppose not. But people have ideas about things like that, and that's why you use initials."

"That's true. At any rate, I didn't ask you to come here so we could talk about me. I want to talk about you."

"You're writing a story about how I was unjustly dismissed from the Rangers, like plenty of other good lawmen? And how a lot of justified convictions got set aside because of some crooked politicians?"

"Whether a politician is a corrupt scoundrel or a sterling example of public service is usually a matter of whether or not you voted for him."

"Not in this case," Braddock said. "Those sons of bitches who ruined the Rangers are all as crooked as a dog's hind leg. Pardon my French."

"I've heard much worse in newspaper offices, I assure you. But I didn't want to meet you so I could write about that. I'm more interested in what you've been doing since you left the Rangers...and what you might do in the future."

Braddock cocked an eyebrow. "What do you mean, what I've been doing since I left the Rangers?"

Elizabeth Jane Caldwell drank some of the coffee and said, "There are all sorts of rumors about you, Mr. Braddock. They say that even though you have no legal right to do so, you're still carrying a Ranger badge and go around pretending that you're a member of the organization so you can chase outlaws. You don't really follow the law anymore. You just dispense justice as you see fit."

"Those are good stories. Not sure anybody could prove there's any truth to them."

"A number of lawbreakers...very bad men, each and every one of them...have wound up dead in the past year, and a man matching your description has been reported to have been in the area each time."

"There are a lot of men who might match my general description."

She reached over to a side table and set the cup on it, then said, "Let's not dance around it. You think you're still a Ranger, or at least you act like one, and you make it your business to go after criminals. That's what I want you to do."

"There some owlhoot in particular you want to sic me onto?"

"I don't have any names. The only thing I know is what happened with the guns."

"What guns?"

Her eyes darkened. "A shipment of a thousand brand-new Springfield rifles, the Krag-Jorgensen model, stolen from a train bound for Fort Bliss, here in El Paso. The holdup took place east of here, between Van Horn and Sierra Blanca."

"Not much out there in those parts."

"Which made it a good place to stop the train, murder the army escort, load those crates full of rifles and ammunition on wagons, and drive off."

"When did this happen?" Braddock asked.

"Two weeks ago."

"I hadn't heard anything about it."

"The railroad and the military are trying to keep it quiet, of course. They don't want people knowing they lost enough rifles to equip a small army."

"A thousand men *is* pretty small when it comes to an army, all right."

"But a thousand well-armed men can do a great deal of damage before they're stopped," Elizabeth Jane Caldwell said.

"True enough, I suppose. If this is supposed to be a big secret, how'd you find out about it?"

She smiled. "I have my own sources and methods, Mr. Braddock. I was in Dallas when I heard rumors about the theft. I've been investigating it ever since."

"A woman could get in big trouble, asking questions about stolen rifles in the wrong places."

"Unfortunately, that's true. A man might be less likely to be suspected."

Braddock sat up straighter and frowned. "That's what you want me to do? Find those rifles? And then tell you so you can write all about it?"

"I thought—"

"A man can get his throat cut for poking into things that aren't his business almost as easy as a woman can." Braddock picked up his hat, stood, stepped over to the side table, and put his cup next to the one she had set aside a few minutes earlier. "Thanks for the coffee and the fifty bucks. You've wasted your newspaper's money, though. Those rifles are probably scattered all over the Southwest by now. I couldn't track 'em down if I tried."

She looked up at him and said, "According to the information I've turned up, that's not the case. The rifles are all still together, pending some sort of deal. I haven't been able to find out where they're being kept or what the plan is, though. But I have a name...Shadrach Palmer."

Braddock frowned. He knew the name. Shad Palmer wasn't in the Rangers' doomsday book, their listing of the most wanted criminals in Texas, but only because nobody had ever been able to get enough proof against the man to charge him with anything. But he was rumored to have his hands in every crooked operation between San Antonio and El Paso, right up to the elbows. He owned a saloon and bawdy house here in El Paso, down close to the river, and was on a first name basis with every desperado on both sides of the Rio Grande.

"You think Shad Palmer is brokering the deal for the guns?"

"I've heard whispers to that effect."

"But they haven't been delivered yet."

"That's right."

Braddock stood there, his expression cold and not giving anything away as he considered what she had told him. Shad Palmer was a very dangerous man, according to everything Braddock had heard. He had never had any dealings with the man or even crossed trails with him, so it was unlikely Palmer would recognize him. That was one point in Braddock's favor.

And as the young woman had said, a thousand Krags could wreak havoc along the border, especially concentrated in the hands of one group, rather than being scattered and sold off piecemeal. He'd never handled one of the rifles, but he knew the army had carried them during the Spanish-American War and in the Philippines.

Elizabeth Jane Caldwell had been right about something else: this sort of affair interested him. But a couple of questions still bothered him.

"Isn't the army looking for these guns?" he asked.

"I'm sure they are, but I haven't been able to find out any specifics." She smiled. "They sort of get quiet out at the fort when I come around."

"And what's your interest in this?"

"Why, I want to write the story, of course—"

"No," Braddock interrupted her. "I saw something else on your face when you explained about that robbery. Something in your eyes, like it hurt you to talk about it. You have a personal connection with this, don't you?"

"I'd prefer not to answer that—"

"And I'd prefer to turn around and walk out of here. All I need is a good reason to do that, and I reckon you keeping secrets from me would qualify."

She stood up and drew in a deep breath. She had to look up to meet his gaze, but there was no give in her. She said, "All right, if you insist. That army escort I mentioned..."

"The troops on the train who were killed in the holdup."

"That's right. They were under the command of a young lieutenant. His name was Peter Caldwell."

Chapter 4

Braddock didn't say anything for a couple of heartbeats. Then he asked, "Your husband?"

"My brother."

"I'm sorry."

"I cried for a day when I heard about it, but not since. Not even at Peter's funeral. I'm more interested in seeing the men responsible brought to justice than I am in grieving. They should pay for what they've done."

"We're in agreement on that. I expect those other soldiers had sisters and wives and parents, too."

"So in a way you'd be working for all of them as well, I suppose."

"I suppose." Braddock set his hat on the table next to the coffee cups. "What else do you know about Palmer's involvement?"

"One of my sources told me Palmer was going to be handling a large transaction involving some goods being taken across the river."

"That could be anything," Braddock said.

"A lot of things come across the border from Mexico to the United States. What goes the other way except guns?"

She had a point there.

"And it's not just the guns," she went on. "Something else is coming across the river to pay for them. I don't know what it is. As you said, there are a lot of possibilities. But that's all I've been able to find out."

Braddock frowned for a moment, then said, "I suppose I could go down to Palmer's place and hang around a little. Maybe ask a few questions without being too obvious about it. No guarantees I'd find out anything, though."

Elizabeth Jane Caldwell started to stand up. "We need to discuss your payment—"

Braddock stopped her by picking up his hat. "We can talk about that later. Give me, let's say, fifty bucks in case I need to throw any money around at Palmer's. I wouldn't even ask for that if I wasn't a mite cash-strapped at the moment."

"The money I sent you..."

"I didn't bring it with me," Braddock said without offering any explanation of what he'd done with the greenback.

"There's not a lot of financial profit in what you do, is there?"

A faint smile touched his lips. "I'm not admitting you're right about me. But my needs don't amount to much, and I get by. There are other things in life besides money."

"Like justice."

Braddock shrugged, put his hat on, and left.

Chapter 5

Braddock had heard of the Palmer House, which he thought was some fancy hotel in Chicago, much like the Camino Real was here in El Paso.

Casa de Palmer, which translated to Palmer House, was a far cry from either of those places, although it was fancy, too, in its own gaudy, sleazy way. Gas lamps lit up the long boardwalk in front of the saloon. Red curtains hung at the sides of the big windows, which offered good views of the cavernous main room. Long mahogany bars ran down both side walls. The back of the room boasted a dance floor and stage where girls in short skirts kicked up their heels. It would have been a stretch to call them dancers, but they tried, making up for what they lacked in talent with exposed flesh.

Poker tables, roulette wheels, faro layouts, and other games of chance filled about half of the floor area. The other half had tables where customers could sit and drink. The light from numerous chandeliers competed with a never-ending, blue-gray haze of tobacco smoke.

In one of the rear corners, next to the stage, was a curving staircase with burgundy carpet on the steps, an ornately carved baluster railing, and a finial on the newel post carved in the shape of a naked woman from the waist up. Those stairs led to the second floor, where another major part of Shadrach Palmer's business was carried out.

Braddock had never been on the second floor of Casa de Palmer. In fact, as he leaned on the bar and sipped from a mug of beer, he tried to remember if he had ever set foot in the building during any of his previous visits to El Paso, back when he'd been a Ranger. He didn't think he had.

He'd heard about the second floor, though. This wasn't some

squalid frontier whorehouse with paper-thin walls between the rooms that sometimes didn't even go all the way to the ceiling. The girls here worked in proper rooms with decent beds instead of cots covered by bug-infested straw ticking. The rooms even had rugs on the floor.

They probably still had a certain disreputable air about them, considering what went on there, but nice enough Palmer could justify charging higher prices. Palmer's real money came from his criminal enterprises, but his saloon and bawdy house turned a nice legal profit, too.

Braddock wore the same dusty range clothes he'd worn on the ride upriver from Esperanza. A gunbelt was snugged around his hips, and his Colt with well-worn walnut grips rode in the holster.

El Paso had a modern police department that frowned on men wearing guns openly like in the old, lawless days, but this close to the border, with the Rio Grande less than two blocks away, nobody tried to enforce that very stringently.

Braddock wasn't going to venture into this part of town with just the derringer, either.

A craggy-faced bartender, one of several drink jugglers working tonight, ambled down the hardwood and frowned at him. Braddock had been working on the beer for a while, and the longer he took drinking it, the less money Shad Palmer made. Braddock figured the bartender was going to tell him to drink up and order another or get out, but before the man could say anything, a commotion erupted on the other side of the room.

"All I'm sayin' is I'd like to know where that third jack came from," a man declared in a loud, angry voice.

"Are you saying that I cheated, sir?"

The room hadn't gone completely quiet after the first outburst, but enough so Braddock had no trouble hearing the question phrased in cool, yet taut tones.

The bartender who'd been about to speak to him had lost interest in him, so Braddock turned to see what was going to happen.

Not surprisingly, the two men who had raised their voices faced each othr across a baize-covered poker table. One was clearly a professional gambler wearing a frock coat and a fancy vest and shirt. His hair was slicked down and he sported a Van Dyke beard.

The man who had asked about the third jack was dressed like a cowboy, with a brown vest over a cotton shirt and an old Stetson pushed back on fair hair. He was approaching middle age, and his face reminded Braddock of a wedge used to split wood.

He was no puncher, despite his clothes. His hands were too soft for that, Braddock noted.

Which meant the holstered gun on the man's hip was probably the tool he used most often.

Braddock took in all those details in the first second after he turned around. By that time the gunman was saying, "I just don't like losin' in a game that ain't on the up and up."

"I deal a fair game," the gambler said, tight-lipped.

"Huh. You couldn't prove it by me."

The gambler stared coldly at him for a moment, then gestured toward the pile of bills and coins in the center of the table.

"Take what you put in the pot and leave," he said. "I want this to be a congenial game, and if you're bent on causing trouble, you're not welcome."

The other man's mouth curved in an ugly grin as he said, "You've got it backwards. I'm the one who tells you to get out. Or have you forgotten who my boss is?"

Anger made the gambler's jaw clench even more. He said, "You don't run this saloon—"

"One word from me is all it's gonna take to get you run out of here, though. Not just this saloon, either. I'll see to it you don't ever set foot in El Paso again."

The gambler put up a bold front, but after a few seconds he sighed and said to the other players, "Help yourselves to the pot, gentlemen. It appears this game has come to an unfortunately abrupt end."

He scraped back his chair, picked up a flat-crowned hat from the table, and stood. Braddock could tell he was trying to muster up as much dignity as he could while he put on the hat and turned toward the saloon's bat-winged entrance.

The gambler was about halfway to the door when the man at the table laughed and said loudly enough to be heard over the growing buzz of conversation, "That's how we deal with damn cheatin' tinhorns around here."

Braddock saw the gambler stop short, saw the way the man's body stiffened, and knew what was going to happen next.

The gambler swung around swiftly. His hand darted under the frock coat to come out clutching a small pistol.

Chapter 6

The gambler's course as he left the saloon had brought him closer to Braddock. Close enough Braddock was able to take two fast steps and bring the beer mug crashing down on the back of the man's head.

The blow made the gambler stumble forward a couple of steps. His arm sagged, and even though the pistol went off, the bullet smacked harmlessly into the sawdust-littered floor right in front of him.

The mug hadn't broken. Braddock hit the gambler again, and this time the blow laid the man out.

The wedge-faced man was on his feet, gun in hand, but he didn't fire. Instead he pouched the iron, snapped his fingers, and pointed at the senseless form on the floor.

A couple of rough-looking men came forward, grabbed the gambler's arms, and hauled him to his feet. The gambler groaned and his head wobbled back and forth as he tried to regain his senses.

As the two men started to half-carry, half-drag the gambler toward the door, the man at the table told them, "Make it clear to him he don't ever show his face around these parts again. Break a finger or two while you're at it, so he won't be so fast to palm those jacks."

"Sure, Dex," one of the men said.

Then the wedge-faced man looked at Braddock and said, "You. C'mere."

Braddock looked down at the beer mug, which was nice and thick and still hadn't shattered. The beer had spilled from it, leaving it empty. He set it on a table where several men were drinking and then walked toward the poker table.

The man greeted him with a cocky grin. "I'd say I'm obliged to you, but I would have killed the son of a bitch, so there wasn't really any need for you to step in."

"Looked to me like he had you shaded," Braddock said. "Maybe I was wrong."

Anger flared for a second in the man's eyes but then faded as he laughed.

"We'll never know," he said. "My name's Dex Wilcox."

"George." That really was Braddock's first name, since the G.W. stood for George Washington.

"First or last?"

"Enough."

"That way, eh? Fine. Let me buy you a drink, George, even though I don't really owe you anything. I'm just the hospitable sort."

"Well, since I lost the rest of my beer trying to keep that tinhorn from shooting you..."

Wilcox jerked his head toward the bar.

As Braddock walked across the room, which was now loud and jovial again, he thought about the man beside him. He had never crossed trail with Dex Wilcox, but he knew the name. Wilcox had a reputation as a gunman and hardcase. Rumor said he had been a member of Black Jack Ketchum's gang of train robbers over in New Mexico Territory.

The things he had said to the gambler made it sound like he now worked for Shadrach Palmer. Braddock had taken note of that at the time, but he hadn't expected to have the chance to make use of the knowledge quite so soon. It was certainly possible Wilcox was working for Palmer, given the saloon owner's rumored connection to all sorts of crimes.

Wilcox signaled to one of the bartenders, who placed two glasses on the bar and then reached underneath it to take out a bottle.

"Hope you don't mind the good stuff," Wilcox said as the bartender poured.

"Well, I may not know what to do with whiskey that doesn't taste like rattlesnake heads and strychnine, but I'll try to manage."

Wilcox laughed. He picked up his drink and raised the glass to

Braddock, who returned the gesture. Both men threw back the liquor.

It was the good stuff, all right. Braddock couldn't help but lick his lips in appreciation.

"I told you." Wilcox nodded toward the gun on Braddock's hip. "Are you as handy with that as you are with a beer mug?"

"Handier, I'd like to think."

"Looking for work?"

"That's why I drifted this way. It's a far piece from Arizona."

"A mite warm over there, is it?"

"It's always hot in Arizona," Braddock said. "You know of any work in these parts?"

Braddock kept his voice casual as he asked the question. He had come here to Casa de Palmer to poke around a little and see if he could pick up any information on those stolen rifles. However, good fortune had put him in the right place at the right time to maybe find out even more. He couldn't appear too eager, though, or he might waste this opportunity.

Wilcox seemed to be thinking about the question Braddock had asked him. After a moment he said, "I know somebody who's always looking to hire good men. You want to meet him?"

"I wouldn't mind," Braddock said.

"Put your glass down, then. He's right upstairs."

Chapter 7

Shadrach Palmer looked more like a shopkeeper than a criminal. A short and pudgy man, he had a few strands of dark hair combed over an otherwise bald pate. He wore a simple dark suit and no gaudy jewelry, just a simple stickpin in his cravat.

The eyes made the difference. Braddock had gazed into a rattlesnake's eyes more than once, and Palmer's eyes had that same flat, dead look to them.

He sat at a writing desk on one side of the suite's sitting room, an open ledger book in front of him. On the other side of the room, a woman relaxed among the cushions of a divan with her legs up. Someone less beautiful would have seemed to be sprawled there, but on her the pose looked elegant.

She was a mulatto, Braddock decided. Just a touch of coffee in the cream of her skin. Waves of dark brown hair framed her lovely face. She wore a silk dressing gown open at the throat just enough to hint at the glories underneath.

It took a man damned dedicated to making money to be studying a ledger book with a woman like that in the room, Braddock thought.

"Got somebody I'd like for you to meet, boss," Dex Wilcox said. "Fella's name is George. That seems to be his only handle."

Palmer didn't get up, but he nodded cordially enough.

"George," he said. "I'm Shadrach Palmer. This is my place."

Braddock returned the nod but didn't take his hat off. He said, "I've heard of you, Mr. Palmer. Pleasure to meet you."

The woman cleared her throat. Palmer smiled, nodded to her, and said, "This is Elise."

Braddock reached for his hat this time. He held it in front of him and said, "It's an honor, ma'am."

"You cowboys are so polite," she said.

"George ain't a cowboy," Wilcox said. "He's in the same line of work I am, from over Arizona Territory way." The gunman paused, then added significantly, "Or at least so he claims."

Braddock's eyes flicked toward him. "Wouldn't be calling me a liar, would you?"

"Nope, just...what do you call it...pleadin' ignorance. After all, George, all we got to go by...is your word."

"You're the one asked me to come up here," Braddock said, not bothering to keep the irritation out of his voice. "Said you wanted me to meet your boss. Why'd you do that if you didn't believe me?"

"Don't get testy, George," Palmer put in. "Dex didn't say he didn't believe you. It's just that sometimes men boast about things they can't back up."

Braddock shook his head slightly and said, "I didn't make any boasts."

Palmer pushed back his chair and stood up. "Let's cut through all this. Why *did* you bring George up here, Dex?"

"You know that gambler Ballantine? He slipped an extra jack into the game I was sittin' in on. I called him on it, he backed down, so I told him to get out. Then as he was leavin', he tried to spin around and gun me." Wilcox didn't say anything about how his words had goaded Ballantine into drawing. He nodded toward Braddock and went on, "George walloped him with a beer mug before he could pull the trigger."

"Saved your life, eh?"

"I wouldn't go that far," Wilcox said, looking annoyed at the suggestion.

Palmer turned to Braddock. "Did the beer mug break?"

"Nope," Braddock said. "It was good and solid."

"Good. If it had, I might have been forced to take the cost out of Dex's wages, since you acted on his behalf, and I'm sure he wouldn't have liked that."

"Blast it!" Wilcox said. "I would have killed that tinhorn before he gunned me."

Palmer chuckled and said, "Take it easy, Dex. We all know what a dangerous gunman you are." He faced Braddock again. "So Dex brought you up here to meet me out of a...sense of gratitude? He thought you would enjoy making my acquaintance?"

"He asked me if I was looking for work, and I told him I was."

"Ah," Palmer said. "I see. Well, I suppose I could always use another bartender, or a man to help unload cases of liquor and sweep out the place—"

Braddock had figured out by now that Palmer was the sort of man who liked to get under people's skin, mostly for the sheer meanness of it. Ignoring Palmer, he turned to Elise, nodded, and interrupted the saloon owner by saying, "It was a real pleasure to meet such a beautiful lady, ma'am. I'll be going now."

He clapped his hat on and turned toward the door of the suite.

"Now wait just a damned minute," Wilcox began. "You can't—"

Palmer silenced him with a lifted hand. "That's all right, Dex. I admire a man with the guts to call my bluff...every now and then." He faced Braddock. "Let's talk plain, shall we?"

"That's the way I like best."

"You do gun work."

"I do."

"And I can always use a man who's quick on the shoot and who isn't overly burdened with, shall we say, moral compunctions."

"Far as I recall, nobody's ever accused me of that. The moral part, I mean. The quick on the shoot part, that's true enough, I reckon."

Palmer put his hands together in front of him, patted them lightly against each other, and said, "There's one good way to find out on both accounts. I want you to kill a man for me."

Chapter 8

Braddock kept his face impassive, but inside he thought this was more than he'd bargained for when he agreed to help Elizabeth Jane Caldwell avenge her brother.

Of course, there was more to it than that. There were all those other soldiers who'd been killed, and the carnage those rifles could wreak if they got into the wrong hands had to be considered, too.

But Palmer seemed to be talking about murder. Braddock might be an outlaw Ranger, but he still tried to uphold the law.

He didn't let any of those thoughts show as they flashed through his mind. Anyway, it wouldn't hurt anything to find out more.

"Who did you have in mind?" he asked coolly.

"There's a man named Larkin. He used to work for me."

Wilcox said, "I've told you, boss, I can take care of Larkin any time you say the word."

"But I haven't said the word, have I?" Palmer snapped at the gunman. "Maybe I've been holding the problem in reserve for just such an occasion as this."

Braddock asked, "What did this hombre Larkin do?"

"He decided he could go out on his own and compete with me." Palmer spread his hands. "I bring in certain...commodities...from across the border and then have them transported to other distribution points."

"You're talking about smuggling." Braddock made a guess. "Opium?"

The flicker of surprise in Palmer's eyes told him he was right, but the man said, "That doesn't matter. What's important is that Larkin betrayed me, and I can't have that. Other people can see what he's done, and if he gets away with it, that will only lead to more trouble for me in the future. It's an annoyance, and I can't have it. Not right now."

Palmer made it sound as if he had a lot bigger deal on the table than just this business with Larkin. Like moving a thousand Krags across the border, maybe?

"Take care of Larkin for me," Palmer went on, "and I'd say you have a job for as long as you want it."

"Answering to you," Braddock said, "or to Wilcox?"

"Now wait just a damned minute," Wilcox said again, clearly displeased that Braddock seemed to be trying to go around him.

"Dex is my chief lieutenant when it comes to matters like this," Palmer said. "You'd answer to him. Do you have any objection to that?"

"None for now," Braddock said.

That didn't do much to mollify Wilcox. He still glared at Braddock when Palmer went on, "Most nights, you can find Larkin at a place over in Juarez owned by a man called Hernandez. I'm not sure it has a name, but Dex can show you where it is. When do you plan to go over there?"

"Nothing wrong with tonight, is there?"

Palmer raised one eyebrow. "So soon?"

"I never believed in wasting time."

"Apparently not." Palmer looked at Wilcox. "Did you have any further plans for the evening, Dex?"

"No, I reckon not." Wilcox's eyes were still narrow with anger as he looked at Braddock.

"Very well, then. Come see me when you get back, George."

"I'll be here," Braddock said.

He turned toward the door. Elise said, "It was nice to meet you, George. Maybe we'll get to know each other better in the future."

Braddock looked back at her and smiled. "Yes, ma'am, maybe."

Palmer frowned a little.

Braddock got out of there. Wilcox followed right behind him.

"You're pretty damned sure of yourself, aren't you?" the gunman said as they walked toward the second floor landing.

"I've never seen any reason not to be."

"Yeah, well, maybe you will tonight. Larkin's generally not by himself. He's liable to have a couple of men with him."

"I take things as they come."

"You'd better not be thinkin' about the woman like that. Palmer wants Larkin dead for hornin' in on his business. He'd want considerably worse for anybody who tried anything with his woman."

"What's considerably worse than being dead?"

"You don't want to know, but trust me...it's out there."

Braddock didn't say anything else as they went down the stairs and crossed the saloon's main room to the entrance. His mind raced.

He had just agreed to go across the river into Mexico and kill one man, maybe more. If Palmer had told the truth about Larkin—and Braddock's gut told him Palmer had—the man smuggled opium across the border, causing a considerable amount of misery among those addicted to the stuff and their families. In all likelihood, Larkin had committed murders as well.

So the world wouldn't miss the man. Braddock often went after that sort, anyway. Considered against the lives in the balance because of those stolen rifles, the deaths of a few criminals didn't mean much.

"You sure you're ready for this?" Wilcox asked when they reached the street.

"I'm ready," Braddock said.

Chapter 9

Their bootheels made echoes in the night as they crossed the wooden bridge spanning the Rio Grande. A lot fewer lights burned in Juarez than in El Paso behind them, but one building not far from the river was well lit, a spawling, two-story adobe with a balcony along the front that overhung its gallery.

"Hernandez's place," Wilcox said as he nodded toward the building.

"A cantina?"

"And a gambling den and a dance hall and a whorehouse." Wilcox laughed. "The boss and Hernandez sort of occupy the same position on each one's side of the river. They ain't partners, exactly, but I guess you could say there's a truce between 'em, for the greater good of both."

"But now Hernandez has thrown in with Larkin?"

"Not yet." Wilcox dug in his left ear with his little finger. "But he might be thinkin' about it. I figure he's waitin' to see what Palmer does about Larkin. In the meantime, he lets Larkin drink and gamble at his place." Wilcox shrugged. "One man's money is as good as another's, I reckon that's the way Hernandez sees it. And I sure as hell can't argue with that idea, either."

They had almost reached the big building. Braddock slowed and looked over at Wilcox.

"You're going to back my play in there?"

Wilcox hooked his thumbs in his gun belt.

"Now, what sort of a test would that be, if I was to save your bacon? You're the one who talked big. Now you got to back it up." Wilcox laughed again. "But don't worry, George. If Larkin or one of his boys kills you, that'll give me all the excuse I need to kill them. The boss gets what he wants, either way."

"And that's what's important, right?"

"As long as he's payin' the wages, it is." Wilcox leaned his head toward the river. "It ain't too late to go back across and say the hell with it. Get on your horse and ride out of El Paso. Nobody'll try to stop you."

"I say I'll do a job, I do it," Braddock replied.

That was the reason he carried a Ranger badge with a bullet hole in it, tucked away now in a hidden pocket cunningly concealed on the back of his gunbelt. He had sworn an oath, and no damned dirty politicians could ever change that.

He pushed open one of the big double doors at the entrance to Hernandez's.

Music rushed out, guitar and piano blending in a staccato rhythm. With it came talk and laughter and tobacco smoke, along with the sharp tang of highly spiced food cooking.

The smell wasn't exactly the same as that of a saloon north of the border, but it had certain similarities. Braddock had been in enough cantinas to recognize it. Here the aromas were just exaggerated, because Hernandez's place was bigger.

Braddock and Wilcox moved inside and let the door swing closed behind them. No one seemed to pay any attention to their entrance, but Braddock would have bet some of the men in the room noted it. He paused to take a look around for himself.

The long mahogany bar stretched most of the way across the back of the room. At either end, a staircase rose to the second floor balcony. The side walls were divided into alcoves where tables could be dimly seen through the beaded curtains hanging over the openings. People could meet in those alcoves to talk, eat, and drink—or whatever else they wanted to do—in private.

The musicians, a piano player and two guitarists, were tucked into a rear corner. Near them, a Mexican girl danced, her colorful skirt swirling around slim brown legs that flashed back and forth in intricate patterns as she moved around a small open area.

Some of the customers watched the dancer and tapped their toes in time to the music, but most remained caught up in their own affairs to which the music and the lithely sensuous girl served as mere background.

All the tables were occupied, and Braddock didn't see many open spaces at the bar.

"Come on," Wilcox said, then added quietly enough that only Braddock could hear him over the hubbub in the room, "I don't see Larkin, but his men are here, so he's somewhere close by."

"Which ones are they?"

"Hatchet-faced scarecrow and a redheaded tree stump at a table to your left."

Braddock let his gaze roam around for a second so it seemed to come back naturally to the table and the men Wilcox indicated. As far as he recalled, he had never seen either of them before, but they looked like the sort of hardcases he had dealt with plenty of times in the past.

"Let's get a drink," Wilcox went on. "Hernandez has the best tequila you'll find this side of Mexico City."

Braddock wasn't that fond of tequila, but he nodded and walked toward the bar at Wilcox's side.

Three bartenders worked behind the hardwood. One of them, a little man with iron gray hair, came over to them and said, "Señores, what can I do for you?"

"Tequila for both of us," Wilcox said. "Where's Hernandez tonight?"

"Señor Hernandez pays my wages, señor. I do not inquire as to his comings and goings."

Wilcox grunted and said, "You can say whether or not you've seen him, can't you?"

"I see only my customers, Señor Wilcox," the bartender said as he poured tequila from an unlabeled bottle into two glasses. The glasses appeared to be clean, Braddock noticed. He'd give Hernandez credit for that.

"All right, fine," Wilcox said. He picked up his drink. So did Braddock.

Before either of them could down the tequila, a scream shrilled over the music and talk and laughter, and when Braddock glanced toward the source of the sound, he saw a young woman running along the second floor balcony, naked as a jaybird.

Chapter 10

Raucous laughter erupted from the place's patrons, especially when a man stumbled out of an open door from one of the second floor rooms, pulling up his pants as he awkwardly gave chase to the girl.

In a place like this, such pursuits might be just part of the play between the soiled doves and their customers. It didn't have to mean anything.

Braddock thought the scream sounded more serious than that, however, and his interest perked up even more when Wilcox said, "That's Larkin."

Braddock knew Wilcox meant the man chasing the whore. Larkin wore trousers and boots but was nude from the waist up, displaying a torso thick with both fat and muscles and covered with coarse black hair like the pelt of a bear. His drooping mustache and the shaggy hair on his head were the same shade.

He got the trousers fastened and loped after the girl. His long legs allowed him to catch her just as she reached the landing of the stairs to Braddock's left. He grabbed her arm and jerked her to a halt, then swung her around and took hold of her other arm as well.

"What the hell's the matter with you?" he roared as he shook her. "I paid for your time. You'll damned well do what I want you to do!"

"N-no, señor!" she gasped. Her head bobbed back and forth from the shaking. "You will injure me! I will die!"

"The hell you will! Even if you do, what's it matter? You're just a whore!"

Braddock saw a couple of hard-faced Mexicans moving toward the stairs. He figured they worked for Hernandez and planned to step in to calm Larkin down and persuade him to leave the girl alone. A whore she might be, but she made money for Hernandez, and that meant she was valuable to him.

Braddock was closer to the stairs than Hernandez's men were. As he put down his untouched drink and stepped away from the bar, he heard Wilcox say, "Hey, what are you—" but then he didn't pay any more attention.

Instead he called up the stairs, "Hey, you big shaggy ape! Let go of her."

Larkin had been drinking. The slur in his voice made that obvious. The insult cut through any fog in his brain, though. His head snapped around toward Braddock.

"What the hell did you say to me, mister?"

"I called you a big shaggy ape and told you to let the girl go. Are you deaf as well as stupid?"

From the corner of his eye, Braddock saw the sly grin that appeared on Wilcox's face. The gunman had figured out that he was baiting Larkin into a fight.

The musicians had stopped playing, and the room was quiet now. The good-natured violence of a man chasing and probably slapping around a whore, which most of the men in here would have accepted without a second thought, had changed into something else, something that might turn deadly serious. Everyone watched to see what would happen next.

With a growl, Larkin shoved the girl away from him. Seizing the opportunity, she sprinted for the room from which she had fled. The door slammed behind her.

"Come up here and say that to me, you son of a bitch," Larkin challenged.

"I'd be glad to," Braddock said. He started up the stairs.

Larkin stood at the landing, grinning and flexing his long, sausage-like fingers. As Braddock neared the top of the stairs, Larkin backed off a little and said, "I ain't armed."

"That's all right. I don't need a gun to deal with gutter trash like you."

Larkin's mouth twisted in a snarl. As soon as Braddock set foot on the landing, Larkin lunged at him, long arms extended, hands reaching to grab and crush and destroy.

Chapter 11

Braddock expected the attack, of course, but Larkin's speed still surprised him. When Larkin had been chasing the girl, he had seemed clumsy, and most men as big as him tended to lumber.

Not Larkin. He barreled at Braddock and crossed the few feet between them like a runaway freight.

Braddock barely had time to twist aside and throw an arm up to block Larkin's intended bear hug. Larkin changed tactics in the blink of an eye, grabbed the arm Braddock used to fend him off, and threw him toward the railing along the edge of the balcony.

Most men would have hit the railing, flipped over it, and fallen. Braddock slapped a hand down on the polished wood and closed it with enough strength to catch himself.

Still, he was dangerously off balance, and if Larkin landed a solid punch on him now, he *would* go over.

Larkin intended to do just that. He swung a looping blow at Braddock's head, again moving faster than it seemed like he ought to be able to. Braddock ducked it, pushed off the railing, and lowered his head. He drove forward and rammed a shoulder into Larkin's chest.

Braddock's rangy body contained a considerable amount of heft and power. The collision sent Larkin reeling back across the balcony to crash into the wall. He rebounded from it, and Braddock displayed his own quickness by darting in and snapping a punch to the bigger man's face.

Blood spurted from Larkin's lips as Braddock's fist landed on them. Larkin grunted and swung his left arm in a backhanded blow. It caught Braddock on the shoulder and knocked him to the side.

Larkin's right fist looped around and dug hard into Braddock's ribs. Larkin followed it an instant later with a straight left that took Braddock just above the heart.

For a moment Braddock thought he was done for. The blow stunned him and left him unable to move.

Larkin sensed victory, too, and grinned.

"I think I'll squeeze your neck hard enough to pop your head right off your shoulders," he said.

The boast was a mistake. Even those few seconds gave Braddock the chance recover a little.

He tried to appear defenseless, though, so when Larkin lunged for Braddock's throat again, he wasn't prepared for his foe to spring out of the way.

Larkin stumbled past Braddock, who clubbed both hands together, lifted them high, and smashed them on the back of Larkin's neck. Larkin doubled over. Braddock grabbed his shoulder, jerked him around, and brought a knee up into Larkin's face. More blood flew as the impact flattened Larkin's nose.

Braddock kicked the smuggler's legs out from under him. Larkin landed in a bloody heap on the balcony. Air rasped through his ruined nose as he breathed heavily.

He wasn't dead, though, and that was what Shadrach Palmer wanted. Braddock couldn't just draw his gun and put a bullet in Larkin's brain. That would be cold-blooded murder.

Luckily—if you could call it that—Larkin wasn't through. He looked up at Braddock with sheer hatred blazing like bonfires in his eyes and reached down to his right boot. He came up with a dagger that had been hidden in the boot. He'd been lying about being unarmed, probably because he had believed he could break Braddock apart with his bare hands.

Now, hurt and on the verge of defeat, he just wanted to destroy his enemy any way he could.

Larkin uncoiled from the floor and came at Braddock, slashing back and forth with the dagger. He didn't even seem to consider that Braddock could have gunned him down, probably because he was so full of rage.

Braddock gave ground until he had retreated about halfway

along the balcony as it ran across the back of the room. He took a risk then, letting Larkin close in on him. The dagger flashed right in front of his eyes, mere inches away. Braddock's hands shot up, closed around Larkin's wrist, twisted and shoved.

Larkin wasn't expecting the move and couldn't stop the dagger in time. The razor-sharp point went in under his chin. Braddock threw his weight against Larkin's wrist and drove the blade deep. He felt it scrape against the spine in Larkin's neck.

Larkin's eyes widened and bulged out. He tried to speak, but only a grotesque gurgle came out. Braddock crowded against him, forcing him back against the railing. Larkin's now nerveless fingers slid loosely off the dagger's handle.

Braddock put both hands against Larkin's chest and pushed.

Larkin went up and over, falling like a stone to land on his back on the bar. Men who had been standing down there craning their necks to watch the fight yelled angry curses and jumped back out of the way. Bottles and glasses and liquor flew. A woman screamed at the sight of Larkin's lifeless body lying there with his arms stretched out on either side of him, the dagger still buried up to the hilt in his throat.

More men scrambled aside, but this time to get out of the line of fire. Braddock glanced toward the hatchet-faced man and the stumpy redhead and saw their gun barrels coming up at him.

Chapter 12

Braddock wasn't in top-notch shape after the battle, and the two gunmen had beaten him to the draw already.

But his hand stabbed down to the gun on his hip, and thankfully it hadn't fallen out during the fracas with Larkin.

The Colt came out of leather with smooth, blinding speed and started roaring a fraction of a second before the shots from below. The redhead had barely pulled his trigger when Braddock's first bullet hammered into his chest and knocked him back over the chair where he'd been sitting.

Hatchet-face got two shots off. The first whipped past Braddock's right ear. The second missed him wide to the left because the gunman had slewed halfway around from the impact of Braddock's second shot. He staggered and pressed his free hand to his chest but couldn't stop the blood bubbling between his fingers. As he tried to lift his gun again for a third shot, Braddock put a round through his head. That dumped him onto the sawdust, dead before he hit.

The redhead was still alive, though. He grabbed hold of the overturned chair and tried to pull himself up. Braddock shot him in the head, too.

That left him with one round in the Colt in case anybody else wanted trouble, but no one seemed to.

The room had cleared out around Larkin's friends. Everybody in the place, customers and employees alike, had pulled back along the walls. Some stared at the carnage, others just seemed annoyed that their night's entertainment had been interrupted.

Braddock heard a little noise to his left and turned. One of the doors stood open a few inches, and a brown face peered out anxiously. The girl said, "Señor Larkin is...is..."

"*Muerto,*" Braddock said.

She closed her eyes, sighed, and crossed herself, which might have seemed more reverent if her bare breasts hadn't been peeking out through the open door, too.

The two men who had been getting ready to step in and deal with Larkin moved over to the dead gunmen and checked on them. The pools of blood around their heads left no doubt they were dead. The two men then turned toward the stairs.

Braddock opened the Colt's cylinder, reached to his shell belt, and started thumbing fresh rounds into the gun. He didn't think Hernandez's men figured on trying anything, but he wanted to be ready if they did.

A glance told him Dex Wilcox was standing off to one side of the room, the glass of tequila still in his hand. He saw Braddock looking at him, grinned, and lifted the glass in a toast of sorts before taking a sip of the fiery liquor.

Down below, the bartenders and a couple of swampers started to gather up the bodies and haul them out. It would take a while to clean up the blood and the other mess, but things would be back to normal in the place fairly quickly.

Assuming no more gunplay erupted. Braddock didn't holster the Colt as the two men reached the top of the stairs and approached him.

"No trouble, señor," one of them said as he raised a hand slightly in a placating gesture. "Señor Larkin brought his fate upon himself, as did his men."

"Is that what the law's going to think?"

A faint smile curved the man's lips. "In this part of Juarez, señor, my employer *is* the law."

"Well, that's good to know, I reckon," Braddock said. "You fellas aren't upset that I horned in? I just can't stand to see an hombre mistreating a woman, even a whore."

"If Señor Hernandez had been here, he would have told us to stop Larkin from hurting the señorita. Larkin might have backed down, or he might have forced us to kill him, too." The man's shoulders rose and fell in an eloquent shrug. "We will never know. But I am sure Señor Hernandez would like to speak with you when he returns. In the meantime, you can drink or gamble or avail yourselves of the other pleasures we have to offer."

An edge of steel under the polite words made it clear Braddock wasn't free to leave here until Hernandez gave the word. That was all right, he decided. Hernandez was tied in with Shadrach Palmer, and Braddock was convinced Palmer had those Krags. Maybe talking to the man was a good idea.

He slid his Colt into its holster and said, "I'll take you up on that, fellas. I—"

"Señor..." a soft voice said behind him.

Braddock looked over his shoulder and saw the girl standing there. She wore a low-on-the-shoulder blouse and long skirt now. Her fingers knotted together nervously in front of her.

"Do not interrupt, Carmen," the man who had been talking to Braddock snapped at her.

"I...I am sorry. I just wanted to thank the señor..."

Acting on impulse, Braddock grinned and said, "I think I know how I want to pass the time until Señor Hernandez gets back."

Again the man shrugged. "As you wish."

"Tell my friend I'll see him later, if he wants to hang around, would you?"

"You mean Señor Wilcox?"

"Yeah."

"You work for Señor Palmer, too?"

"That's right," Braddock said, not bothering to explain that he'd been sent over here on a provisional basis, with his assignment being to kill Larkin for double-crossing Palmer. Let them think the deaths of Larkin and his men had been just an unfortunate turn of events.

"Very well. Enjoy your time with Carmen. We will let you know when Señor Hernandez arrives. Would you like a bottle of tequila sent up?"

"I think that's a mighty good idea," Braddock said.

After everything that had happened, poor little Carmen looked like she could use a drink.

Chapter 13

When the two of them were alone in Carmen's room, the girl looked down at the threadbare rug on the floor next to the bed and said, "Anything you want to do with me, señor, it is all right. I owe you my life."

"I don't know about that," Braddock said. "Hernandez's men would stepped in and done something about Larkin."

Carmen shook her head. "Even if they made him leave me alone tonight, Señor Larkin would have caught me some other night. He would not have forgotten. He is like a dog. Once he has gotten his jaws on something, he will not let go."

"Yeah, he was a son of a bitch, all right," Braddock said with a smile.

"He has hurt other girls in the past, very badly. I have heard stories about him..."

"Well, he won't hurt anybody else." Braddock put a couple of fingers under her chin. "Why won't you look at me?"

He urged her head up. When she blinked at him, he saw tears shining in her dark eyes.

"I am so...so ashamed!" she burst out. She stepped back, put her hands over her face, and sobbed.

Braddock frowned. Like most men, crying women made him distinctly uncomfortable. He didn't know if it would be better to put his arms around Carmen or keep his distance.

A soft knock sounded on the door. Braddock said, "Why don't you sit down on the bed?" and turned to answer it. He rested his right hand on the butt of the Colt and used his left to open the door.

The gray-haired bartender from downstairs stood there holding a tray with a bottle of tequila and two glasses on it.

"Perhaps this time you will actually get to enjoy your drink, señor," he said. He ignored Carmen crying quietly as she perched on the edge of the bed.

"Here's hoping." Braddock slipped a silver dollar from his pocket, handed it to the bartender, and took the tray.

"Gracias, señor."

"Is my friend still downstairs?"

"Señor Wilcox? Sí. I think he intends to wait for you. He is playing poker with some other men."

That came as no surprise. Wilcox seemed to like gambling.

Braddock closed the door with his foot and set the tray on a small table. He poured a couple of inches of tequila into one of the glasses and carried it over to Carmen.

"Here," he told her. "Drink this."

She took the glass, gulped down the liquor, gagged a little, and shuddered.

"Not used to drinking, are you?"

"I am...not used to...many things," she said. "All of this..." She moved a hand in a vague gesture to indicate the room around them. "This is new to me."

Braddock glanced around the spartanly furnished room. It held a bed, a single chair, the table with a basin of water and a cheap oil lamp on it. He had seen worse, though. The floor had a rug on it, and a thin curtain hung over the single window, open to let in a little breeze. As a whore's room, it wasn't that bad.

"You don't have to be ashamed," he said. "Folks do what they have to do in order to survive."

"You do not understand, Señor...?"

"George."

"Señor George. It was not my choice to come here. I was taken from my village and *brought* here. Stolen with all the others by evil men."

"Others?" Braddock repeated.

Carmen nodded. "More than two dozen women and girls, some as young as ten years old." She swallowed hard. "And now we are all doomed."

Chapter 14

Braddock had to pour another drink for her before she could go on with the story. She didn't shudder as much as she downed the liquor this time.

She told him about the dawn raid on the village of Santa Rosalia where she had lived with her family.

"So many of the men were killed, including my father," she said in a voice hollow with grief. Braddock saw the shock and horror of that morning on her face as she relived it in her memory. "Then they rounded up the women and put us onto carts like nothing more than...than sheep. We were nothing but livestock to those terrible men."

She was right about that, Braddock thought.

"Then their leader, he...he pointed to me and had one of his men bring me to him. That man, Gonsalvo, tore my clothes from me and left me naked and ashamed."

"This Gonsalvo, he was their leader?" Braddock didn't know the name.

Carmen shook her head. "No, no, Hector Gonsalvo was the, how do you say it, the segundo...the lieutenant. The leader was Martin Larrizo."

That name rang a faint bell for Braddock. He thought for a moment and dredged up the details from his brain.

The Rangers had suspected Larrizo of being involved with several raids across the border into Texas to steal cattle and loot isolated ranches. As far as they knew, he was just a minor bandido.

Maybe Larrizo had in mind becoming something bigger, and the mass kidnapping of the women of Santa Rosalia was a start.

"Go on," he told Carmen.

She frowned at him in confusion. "Why do you ask me these

questions? Why do you want to know about me? I thought we would..."

"I can see how upset you are. I just figured you might like to talk a little and tell me about it. I'm a nice hombre, after all."

She peered intently at him for a long moment, then shook her head.

"No. You are not an evil man, I can sense that. But you are hard and dangerous and...and not nice."

Braddock laughed and said, "I'm sure some folks would agree with that last part. But I still want to know about what happened to you."

So far, he didn't have any idea if Carmen's story had anything to do with the mission that had brought him to Juarez, but again, connections existed between Palmer and Hernandez, so that meant Hernandez's other activities might be involved, too.

"It is an ugly thing," Carmen went on. "Larrizo took me as his...his prize. His men were not allowed to touch the other prisoners, and if they did, Larrizo or Gonsalvo would kill them. Gonsalvo told the men this. But Larrizo had his way with me. Until then I...I had never been with a man before. He said he had to...sample the merchandise."

She had handed the empty glass back to Braddock after downing the tequila. His fingers tightened on it in anger until he thought it might break.

He suppressed that fury for the moment and told her, "I'm sorry you had to go through that, Carmen, I really am. Where are the other women now? Are they still together?"

"I do not know. I think...maybe they are. Larrizo and his men, they brought us to a place...They blindfolded us so we could not see where we were going...and when they took the blindfolds off, we were all in a room with stone walls and no windows and only one door which was always guarded. They gave us food and water and kept us there."

"You weren't with Larrizo anymore?"

She shook her head and said in a small voice, "I think he had grown tired of me."

"But he didn't take any of the other women to replace you?"

"No. We were all there."

"How'd you wind up here?"

"Gonsalvo came and got me. He put a...a bag of some kind over my head this time, instead of blindfolding me, and brought me away from there. The next thing I knew, I was here at Señor Hernandez's."

Braddock tugged at his earlobe as he frowned in thought. He said, "Wait a minute. Tell me *everything* you remember about being taken out of that place where the prisoners are kept."

"Why?" she asked. "I do not understand—"

"It might be important," Braddock said. He wasn't quite sure why, either, but his gut told him to find out as much as he could.

Carmen took a deep breath. "There is nothing to remember. Gonsalvo covered my head, and then he held my arm so tight it hurt, and he took me upstairs and lifted me onto a horse. We rode and rode, and then he took me down from the horse and we went up more stairs, and then we were here. I have seen little but the inside of this room...and the men who come to me here...since."

The wheels of Braddock's brain turned faster now. Carmen didn't seem to realize it, but she had told him something. When Gonsalvo had left the prison with her, they had gone up some stairs, Carmen had said, and gotten on a horse.

That meant the other women and girls were being kept below ground level, probably in a cellar. That would match the description of no windows and only one door.

But a cellar where? Right now, that was impossible to answer, and Braddock still wasn't sure why he needed to know, other than the fact he didn't like the idea of all those women ultimately facing the same fate as Carmen.

Braddock rubbed his chin and asked, "Did Gonsalvo say anything when he brought you here?"

"He...he made a joke, or at least acted like he thought it was funny. He said someone else wanted to see what they would be getting for their money. He said for me to get used to it. But I think he was angry, too, that he and the rest of Larrizo's men had been ordered to leave the prisoners alone."

Braddock didn't say anything. A picture had begun to form in his head, a picture that would explain everything he had come across so far.

It was a damned ugly picture, too.

But before he could ponder that any more, a knock sounded on the door. Braddock glanced toward it, then looked back at Carmen and said, “Take your clothes off.”

Chapter 15

She gave him that confused look again and said, "I had started to think you did not want—"

"Now," he told her in a quiet but urgent voice.

She stood up, peeled the blouse over her head, pushed the skirt down over flaring hips and kicked out of it.

The covers were already pulled back on the bed. Braddock motioned toward it.

"Don't mention what we talked about to the other women who work for Hernandez," he told her.

"I don't talk to them."

"Good."

He wished he could tell her to have faith, that everything would be all right. He wished he could promise he'd see to it.

But he didn't know any of that for certain and didn't want to give her false hope. She had survived for this long. Maybe she could hold out for a while longer.

Another knock sounded on the door, a sharper rapping this time. Braddock turned toward it and glanced over his shoulder at the bed. Carmen sprawled on top of the covers, knees up and legs slightly spread.

Braddock opened the door. The pair of Hernandez's men stood there, just as he expected.

"Señor Hernandez is back," the talkative one—if you could call him that—said. "He wishes to see you, as I knew he would."

"Fine," Braddock said. He straightened his hat a little, as if he had just put it on. He saw the men look past him at Carmen lying on the bed. Their scrutiny probably embarrassed her, but that couldn't be helped. He turned slightly and told her, "Vaya con Dios, señorita," then went out and closed the door behind him.

From what he could see of the main room below, things had

indeed gone back to normal. Wilcox wasn't in his line of sight, but he supposed the gunman was still playing poker. The musicians played another sprightly tune for the lissome young woman to dance to.

The hard-faced pair led him to a door in the far corner. One of them opened it and revealed a short hallway with another door at the end of it. There was an apartment at the back of the building, Braddock realized. It probably served as Hernandez's private quarters.

One of the men knocked on the far door, opened it, and ushered Braddock into a sitting room every bit as luxurious as Shadrach Palmer's on the other side of the river. They really were two sides of the same coin, Braddock thought...except Hernandez didn't look like a dumpy little storekeeper at first glance.

Hernandez was taller and more powerfully built than Palmer, with a full head of dark brown hair lightly touched with silver here and there. He was clean-shaven except for long sideburns. Braddock had a hunch women considered him very handsome.

Hernandez appeared to have been riding recently. A fine film of trail dust clung to his boots and whipcord trousers and short, dark brown jacket. He wore no visible gun, but a slight bulge under the jacket might be a pistol in a shoulder holster, Braddock noted.

"The gringo, Señor Hernandez," one of the men who had brought him in murmured.

Hernandez's eyes regarded Braddock from under prominent brows. He said, "You are the one who killed Calvin Larkin?"

"I didn't know his name," Braddock said, maintaining the fiction that Larkin hadn't been his target all along, "but yeah, I reckon I'm him. My handle is George."

"From what I am told of the incident, you are a very dangerous man, Señor George. You killed not only Larkin but the two men who work with him. All three of them had considerable blood on their hands, I suspect, and would not be easy to kill."

"I wouldn't know about that," Braddock said with a faint shake of his head. "I haven't been in El Paso for long."

"You are not in El Paso *now*. You are in Juarez. And in Juarez, *I* am the law."

"So I've heard. I was protecting one of your employees when I stepped in, though. That ought to be worth something."

Hernandez blew out his breath and said, "A prostitute. Less than nothing. Larkin was a potential...business associate."

"I'd apologize for ruining your plans, but I still say the son of a bitch had it coming to him."

"No doubt. Calvin Larkin was a very unpleasant man. And if I were to ever do business with him, it would have been in the future, not now. Now I already have arrangements in place. So in a way, Señor George, I suppose I owe you my thanks. You have...simplified my life, let us say."

"Always glad to be of help," Braddock said dryly.

Hernandez looked at him for a second, then laughed.

"I think I like you," he said. "You have a certain boldness about you. You remind me of me. I'm told you came in tonight with Dex Wilcox."

It wasn't really a question, but Braddock said, "That's right," anyway.

"So you work for Señor Palmer as well."

"Just started."

"And while waiting for me, you spent time with Carmen?"

"Yep."

"You enjoyed your time with her?"

"Very much so."

"Good. You can become accustomed to such pleasures. I'm sure that we will be seeing each other again."

Hernandez turned away in obvious dismissal. The other two men moved up closer to Braddock, who said, "Buenas noches, Señor Hernandez."

Hernandez just grunted and didn't say good night.

The men escorted Braddock out. Once they reached the balcony, he said, "I reckon since your boss gave his seal of approval to what happened, I'm free to go."

"Certainly. And you are welcome back here."

"Obliged for the hospitality," Braddock said. He started down the stairs.

The picture in his mind was even clearer than before, and just as ugly as ever.

Chapter 16

Braddock spotted Wilcox as he went down the stairs. The gunman slouched at one of the tables, playing poker with four other men. Wilcox must have seen him, too. He looked at the cards in his hand, shrugged, and threw them in, folding so he could leave the game. He stood up, nodded to the other players, and then headed for the stairs to meet Braddock at the bottom of them.

"Well, I see Hernandez didn't have you taken out into the desert and left in a shallow grave," Wilcox said with a grin.

"I got the feeling he wasn't too happy about me killing Larkin," Braddock said. "He hadn't decided yet about double-crossing Palmer and throwing in with Larkin."

"Then you came along and made up his mind for him."

"He said pretty much the same thing."

"That's what the boss wanted," Wilcox said. "Hernandez probably suspects Palmer might have sent you here to get rid of Larkin, but the way it all played out, he can't be sure about that. For the sake of keepin' the peace, he'll give Palmer the benefit of the doubt. You wound up doin' a mighty fine job, George. The boss is gonna be pleased."

"I'm glad to hear it," Braddock said. "I could use a nice steady job for a while."

"Until the heat dies down enough in Arizona for you to go back, eh?"

"Who knows?" Braddock said. "I might decide I like it in Texas."

Wilcox's grin slipped a little, but he didn't say anything except, "Come on. Let's get back across the river."

They left the place and walked toward the bridge a few blocks away. In the warren of alleys and shacks spreading out on both sides of the main street, a dog barked and a woman cried. Typical nighttime sounds, Braddock thought. He wished there had been some way for him to take Carmen out of Hernandez's, but he hadn't been able to think of any that wouldn't threaten his plans.

He decided to probe a little more and said, "You know, I got to thinking about it, and I believe I've heard of you, Dex. You used to ride with Black Jack Ketchum, didn't you?"

"What if I did?" Wilcox asked, his voice sharp with sudden suspicion.

"I don't mean any offense," Braddock went on. "In fact, I've always admired fellas who could pull off stopping a train and holding it up. Seems like that would take an awful lot of both guts and brains."

Wilcox grunted and sounded somewhat mollified as he said, "You're damn right about that. "The Reno brothers and then Jesse and his boys showed us all how it's done, 'way back when, but since then the railroads have gotten better about protectin' their trains...and fellas like me have gotten even better at holdin' 'em up."

"Must be sort of tiresome for you, hanging around town like this and running errands for Palmer when you're used to bigger and better things."

Wilcox's voice had a knife edge to it again as he said, "Don't ever mistake me for an errand boy. Palmer's got a damned big deal in the works, and he never could've pulled it off without me. He knows it, too."

"I'm sure he does," Braddock said. He'd had a hunch Wilcox had been in charge of the train robbery that had netted Palmer the shipment of rifles. Now Wilcox's boasting made him certain of it. "What's this big deal you're talking about?"

"You'll find out soon enough if the boss hires you. After tonight, I don't reckon there's much doubt about that. In fact, once he hears about the slick way you handled that whole Larkin business, he'll be really happy. You'll be his fair-haired boy, I'd say."

Braddock shook his head as they reached the bridge over the Rio Grande and started out onto it.

"I wouldn't go that—"

Before he could continue, Wilcox yanked out his gun, lunged at Braddock, and chopped at his head with the revolver.

Chapter 17

From the corner of his eye, Braddock saw Wilcox make his move. It wasn't a complete surprise. Wilcox had seen what the newcomer could do and feared that given time, Braddock would worm his way into Wilcox's position in Palmer's hierarchy of hired guns.

Things probably never would have gotten that far, but Wilcox had no way of knowing that.

Braddock twisted aside, getting out of the way of the blow so it hammered down on his right shoulder instead of crushing his hat and maybe busting his skull.

It was bad enough getting hit the way he did, because it made his arm and hand go numb—and that was his gun hand.

He jerked back and swung his left arm at Wilcox's gun, knocking the revolver aside for a second. That gave Braddock enough time to kick Wilcox in the belly. Wilcox groaned and staggered back a couple of steps, but he didn't drop the gun.

The two of them were alone on the bridge. A half moon floated overhead, giving them enough light to see each other. Wilcox straightened up from the kick, bared his teeth in a grimace, and said, "I didn't want to shoot you, George—"

"No, you just figured you'd stove in my skull and drop me in the river to drown," Braddock said. "Then you could tell Palmer I went off on my own somewhere after we left Hernandez's together, and you didn't know what happened to me after that. If anybody found my corpse, they'd just think some thief jumped and robbed me before dumping me in the river."

"It could'a happened that way."

"Then I'd never have a chance to take over your spot, would I?"

Wilcox laughed, but it sounded hollow. "You think I'm scared of you, George? You're just a two-bit hardcase. You got lucky against Larkin and his boys!"

"You saw me shoot it out with those two," Braddock said. "That look like luck to you?"

Wilcox snarled an obscenity and jerked his gun up, obviously not caring any more about drawing attention with a shot.

Braddock dived to the side as Colt flame bloomed in the night. He felt the bullet rush past his ear. He tried to slap at the Colt on his hip, but his right arm still hung limp and unresponsive. Under different circumstances he might have worried that Wilcox had broken his arm.

Now he just worried about staying alive.

Wilcox was already tracking the gun to the side for another shot. Braddock dove at his knees and took his legs out from under him. Wilcox fell on top of him. Braddock rolled desperately to throw Wilcox off of him and grabbed for Wilcox's gun with his left hand.

Braddock missed the revolver but got hold of Wilcox's wrist. He slammed it down hard on the bridge planks. Wilcox cried out in pain. Braddock drove his gun hand down again, and this time the weapon slipped out of Wilcox's fingers and skidded away.

Braddock scrambled after it. He was a decent shot with his left hand, and it was faster and easier to scoop up Wilcox's gun than it would have been to reach across his body and draw his own Colt.

His fingertips had just brushed the gun butt when Wilcox tackled him from behind. Braddock went down. The heel of his hand struck the gun and caused it to skid even farther away.

Wilcox smashed a fist into Braddock's right kidney. Braddock gritted his teeth against the pain, writhed over, and brought his left elbow up into Wilcox's face. That knocked Wilcox over onto his back. Braddock went after him and dug a knee into his groin. Wilcox gasped curses and curled up around the agony.

Braddock climbed wearily to his feet. His right arm began to tingle as feeling inched back into it. Maybe it wasn't hurt too bad after all, he thought.

He looked around, spotted the dark shape of the gun lying on the bridge a few yards away, and stumbled over to it. He bent down to pick it up with his left hand, turned and steadied himself to cover Wilcox.

The question now was what he should do with the gunman and train robber. After this attempt on his life, he couldn't ever trust Wilcox again.

But he couldn't just waltz into the El Paso police station, turn Wilcox over to the lawmen, and tell them how Wilcox had had a hand in holding up that train, killing those soldiers, and stealing all those army rifles. The whole story was too complicated, and he was wanted, too, after all. The police would hold him while they tried to sort everything out, and word might get to the Rangers that he was locked up.

The simplest thing would be to do to Wilcox what Wilcox had figured on doing to him. Bust his head open and dump him in the river, then go back to Palmer and plead ignorance as to Wilcox's fate. Palmer might suspect he'd had something to do with the disappearance, but nobody would be able to prove anything.

It was too bad he didn't have a place he could stash Wilcox for a while...

Braddock considered all those options as he took a couple of steps toward Wilcox, and he was still trying to figure out what to do when Wilcox suddenly stopped groaning and rolled over toward him. Wilcox's arm came up and flame spouted from the muzzle of the derringer he'd had hidden somewhere in his clothes.

The derringer made a loud pop, like somebody had clapped two boards together. Braddock felt the bullet rip into him. He dropped Wilcox's gun, reeled back against the bridge railing, and toppled over it.

The fall lasted only a couple of heartbeats before Braddock struck the surface of the Rio Grande and went under, but it seemed longer than that.

Chapter 18

It would have been easy to surrender to the embrace of the warm, gently flowing water. Braddock could just let himself float away downriver...

The Rio Grande was only about eight feet deep here. Braddock's left hand touched the sandy bottom. He righted himself and kicked with his legs. He heard a couple of muffled booms and knew Wilcox was shooting at him...or at least shooting where Wilcox thought he was.

Braddock was already twenty feet downstream. He kept going that way, swimming underwater and trying to disturb the surface as little as possible. While he was falling from the bridge, he had sucked in as deep a breath as he could, so he didn't want to come up where Wilcox could still see him.

His right arm had started working well enough again he could stroke clumsily with it. That kept him from swimming in circles, anyway. The pain in his side where the bullet from Wilcox's derringer had struck him wasn't too bad. He managed to put it aside and not pay any attention to it.

He never had figured out what to do with Wilcox after the gunman tried to kill him, but that dilemma had vanished in the pop of the derringer. The boot was back on the other foot. Wilcox would have to go back to Shad Palmer and claim ignorance of the new man's whereabouts. Palmer might be annoyed by "George's" disappearance, but Larkin was dead and that was the main thing he had wanted out of this night.

Even as he was falling into the Rio Grande, Braddock had realized it might be to his advantage to stay dead for a while.

That required not actually dying by drowning, of course.

He didn't hear any more shots. Wilcox might have left the bridge and started running along one of the river banks, looking for him. Braddock had to risk that, because his lungs burned from lack of air.

He stopped kicking and let his legs drop, not a problem because his boots pulled them down. He stroked with his arms and lifted himself enough that his mouth and nose came out of the water. Trying not to be too noisy about it, he gulped down a breath.

He couldn't float very well, not fully dressed and with his boots on, but he managed to tread water and let the river's sluggish current carry him slowly downstream. Braddock looked from side to side, searching the banks for movement. He didn't see any, but that didn't mean he was in the clear yet.

His side began to ache. He put that out of his mind, let himself sink beneath the water, and began swimming again. He stayed under as long as he could, then came up for air again.

No bullets came screaming out of the night.

Wilcox had to believe he was dead. More than likely, he had left some blood on the bridge, and if Wilcox saw that, he would know his shot had struck Braddock. The way Braddock had gone right into the river and not come up again sure made it look like he was dead.

Braddock wanted Wilcox to keep on thinking that. To help insure the assumption, he stayed in the river and let it carry him downstream until he was just too weak and exhausted to manage anymore. Sensing that he might pass out and drown for real, he struggled to the southern bank and crawled out onto the sand.

The scattered lights of El Paso and Juarez lay to his right, at least a mile away. Where he had left the river was nothing but sand and scrub brush, maybe a rattlesnake or two hunting in the darkness. Braddock hoped he wouldn't run into any of them. He pulled himself farther from the water.

Muffled hoofbeats sounded in the distance. Braddock listened and could tell they were coming closer. Muttering curses under his breath, he came up on hands and knees and moved as fast as he could toward a cluster of mesquite trees barely larger than bushes. The shadows were thick among them, though, and that was all Braddock cared about at the moment.

He thought about those rattlesnakes again as he crawled among the mesquites. He didn't hear any warning buzzes, though, just the faint clicking as night breezes blew mesquite beans against each other. In the thickest shadows, he bellied down in the sand to wait.

The approaching rider might be Dex Wilcox, looking for him, but logically Braddock knew it was probably someone else, someone who had nothing to do with him. He waited, barely breathing. His gun still rested in its holster, but he wouldn't trust it to fire properly after having been immersed in the river for so long.

The soft, thudding hoofbeats moved past him, thirty or forty yards from the mesquite thicket where he sprawled. In the light from the moon and stars, he saw the rider's silhouette topped with a broad-brimmed, steeple-crowned sombrero, nothing like the Stetson Wilcox wore. Braddock heaved a sigh of relief as the man rode on.

He was safe, but only for the moment. Not only that, but he still didn't know how badly wounded he was or how much blood he had lost. He had been forcing his battered body to go on, but that couldn't continue much longer.

He sat up and reached down to his right side where the bullet had struck him. The river had soaked his shirt, of course, so he couldn't tell from feeling it how much blood had leaked from the hole he found. A grimace pulled his lips away from his teeth as he probed the wound and the area around it.

A few inches back from the bullet hole, he found a hard lump under his skin. That was it, he thought. The bullet hadn't penetrated very far, skimming along his side until it came to a stop. He was surprised it hadn't come on out. The derringer must have been a small caliber weapon not packing much punch.

Braddock reached into his pocket and found the clasp knife he carried. As he opened it, he thought about how awkward this impromptu surgery was going to be. He didn't want to haul that slug around inside him, though. That was a good way to get blood poisoning. He gritted his teeth and started digging at the bullet in his side, trying to get the tip of the blade underneath it.

Suddenly, a vision of his father appeared before him.

"It's just a damn splinter," Pa said, brandishing a giant Bowie knife. "Now hold still and lemme take it outta there. Can't leave it in. It'll rot your whole hand off. Don't want that, do ya?"

George swallowed hard and said, "No, sir." But he saw the way his father's hands trembled and knew Pa had been drinking, and he couldn't stop a tear from trickling down his cheek.

"You know how many bullets I've taken outta men? Hell, I've carved bullets outta my own hide! What're you gonna do, one of these days when you're a Ranger and you're out in the middle o' nowhere by yourself and some damn greaser shoots you? You gonna just lay down and die, or are you gonna take that bullet out and live?" Pa let out a contemptuous snort. "Hell, what am I talkin' about? They'll never take a scared little piss-ant like you in the Rangers. Now hold still—"

George screamed as the tip of the Bowie lanced into his palm, gouging for the splinter...

The bullet popped out of his side and thudded to the sand. Braddock followed it an instant later, collapsing as he passed out.

Chapter 19

The mesquite branches threw a latticework of shadows over his face when he woke up, but the sun still shone brightly enough through them to make him wince and turn his head away from the stabbing glare.

The movement made his stomach roil and his head throb for a moment, but the feeling passed. He sat up slowly, stiff, sore muscles complaining as he did so. His injured side caught and twinged sharply. He sucked in his breath.

The mesquite beans rattled to his left. He looked in that direction and saw a small brown face peering at him through the branches. A boy, eight or ten years old, jumped back when he saw Braddock looking at him.

"Don't be afraid," Braddock told him in Spanish. "I won't hurt you."

"You are not dead," the boy said.

"No. Halfway there, maybe, but no further."

The boy started to back off.

"Wait," Braddock said. "Don't run away. Do you live near here?"

"My father's farm is that way." The boy pointed southeast along the Rio Grande.

"Your father...does he drink tequila or mescal or pulque?"

A look of understanding appeared on the boy's face. "I thought you were hurt," he said. "Now I see you have had too much to drink."

He looked and sounded a mite too world-weary for his years, Braddock thought.

"I *am* hurt." Braddock turned a little and pulled up his shirt so the boy could see both the bullet hole and the wound where Braddock had cut out the slug. "I need the tequila for medicine, not for drinking."

The youngster frowned and said, "My apologies, señor—"

"That's all right," Braddock assured him. "Do you have a horse?"

"A burro."

"Can you get him and bring him back here?"

The boy nodded and started to turn away, then paused and said, "My name is Alphonso."

"I'm George."

"Wait there."

"Thank you," Braddock said. In truth, he couldn't do anything *except* wait. He was too weak to get up and wander off by himself.

Alphonso didn't come back for a long time, and Braddock had just about decided he wasn't coming back when the youngster walked up to the thicket leading a short-legged burro. Braddock had been saving what little strength he had. He used it now to crawl over to the burro and reach up to grasp the animal's harness.

Alphonso took hold of Braddock's other arm to help him. With all three of them working at it—although in truth, the burro didn't do anything but stand there—Braddock got to his feet.

"Have you told your mother or father about me?" he asked.

Alphonso shook his head. "My father and my brothers are working in the fields. My mother is home with my little sisters."

For a moment, Braddock wondered why the boy wasn't working in the fields, too, but then he saw the unnatural twist to Alphonso's left leg. It didn't seem to keep him from getting around, but he would have a difficult time putting in a full day's work.

"What's your mother going to do when you show up with me? She won't shoot me, will she?"

Alphonso looked horrified at the idea. "No, señor! She is a good woman who prays every day to the Blessed Virgin. You are injured. She will care for you."

"I can use it," Braddock muttered. "Let's go."

He leaned on the burro and forced his legs to work. They walked slowly along the river with Alphonso leading the burro.

Braddock hoped Dex Wilcox or one of his other enemies didn't happen to come along. He wouldn't be able to put up much of a fight, and Alphonso would be in the line of fire.

No one seemed to be around, though, and after a little while the adobe jacal where Alphonso and his family lived came in sight. Braddock saw some younger children playing outside but no sign of the boy's mother.

"Are you a bad man?" Alphonso asked.

"What?"

"You have been shot." As if that explained the question.

"A lot of people who aren't bad get shot. It's the bad people who shoot them."

"So a bad man shot you?"

Braddock thought about Dex Wilcox and said, "A very bad man."

"That's all right, then. Mama will help you."

Braddock hoped so, because even this short walk had him just about at the end of his rope again.

Because of that, he couldn't do anything except stop and stand there when a woman stepped around a corner of the jacal holding a pitchfork and looking like she wanted to ram it right through his guts.

Chapter 20

Braddock wondered idly if she was part Yaqui. Her face was fierce enough for that to be the case.

Or maybe she just looked like that because she thought she was defending her home and family.

"Alphonso, what have you done?" she demanded.

"It's all right, Mama. This man was lying in the mesquites, hurt. I thought he was dead at first, but he isn't. He's been shot and needs some of Papa's tequila as medicine."

The woman looked at Braddock. "You have been shot?"

"Yes, ma'am," he said. Bracing himself on the burro, he half-turned and pulled up his shirt again to reveal the wounds.

"Where are the men who shot you?"

"It was just one man, and he's back in El Paso, I reckon. I'm pretty sure he thinks I'm dead."

The woman frowned and said, "I will not have you bringing trouble into my house."

"Well, then," Braddock said, feeling himself growing weaker, "I'll just sit out here, then..."

His head spun, and he would have fallen if Alphonso hadn't caught hold of his arm. The woman looked indecisive for a second, then she leaned the pitchfork against the jacal's adobe wall and hurried forward. She took Braddock's other arm, and they helped him to a three-legged stool near the doorway.

"Sit here," she told him after they had lowered him carefully onto the stool.

"Yes, ma'am. I don't really feel like getting up and doing a jig."

The thought of that made him laugh. The sound of the laughter made him realize he was lightheaded and not himself at all. The sun was hot as it beat down on him, or else a fever had hold of him. Maybe both.

The three little girls, all younger than Alphonso, gathered a few yards away and stared at Braddock. He was just loco enough at the moment he was tempted to say "Boo!" at them, but he knew if he did that, they would scream and run off and their mama might be mad at him. He didn't want that.

She came back with a basin of water and a rag in one hand, a clay cup in the other.

"Can you hold this to drink?" she asked as she held out the cup.

"I don't know, but I'll try."

"Alphonso, help him."

With the boy's hand on the cup, too, to steady it, Braddock lifted it and sipped the clear liquid inside. The fiery bite of it told him it was tequila.

"Don't drink it all," the woman said. "I'll use it to clean the wounds, after I have washed them."

"Yes, ma'am, that's just what I had in mind."

She lifted his shirt and used the wet rag to swab away the blood that had flowed from the holes and dried after Braddock emerged from the river. Then she squeezed out the rag, took the cup, soaked the cup in the tequila, and pressed it deep into the bullet hole.

Braddock said, "Ahhhh," and leaned his head back, baring his teeth.

The woman repeated the process with the hole Braddock had made to get the slug out. It hurt just as bad, but he expected it this time and didn't react quite as strongly.

"Come inside," the woman said. "You must lie down."

"I *am* mighty tired."

"You must lie on your side so I can pour tequila into the wounds."

"Oh. Well, that's gonna hurt."

Alphonso said, "And Papa will say it is a waste of good tequila."

"Never mind what your papa will say," the woman snapped. "Help the gringo."

With their assistance, Braddock hobbled inside and lay down on a bunk with a straw mattress. It felt good and Braddock might have dozed off right away, except the woman made good on her word and carefully tilted the cup to let raw tequila run into the holes in Braddock's hide. He didn't yell out loud, but he didn't miss it by much.

The burning pain still filled him enough he was barely aware of it when the woman slid the Colt from its holster. Braddock wanted to object. His instincts rebelled at the idea of anybody taking his gun.

But he didn't figure she planned to use it against him. If she'd wanted him dead, she could have let him fall down in front of her house and lie there until the sun and the fever killed him. She could get that pitchfork and stab him full of holes. She didn't need to shoot him.

Through slitted eyes, he saw her place the revolver on a table.

"Stay away from the gun," she told Alphonso in a stern voice. "Do not touch it. Do not even get near it."

"Yes, Mama," the boy said.

She turned to Braddock with her mouth open to say something else to him.

He didn't know what it was, because just then he passed out again.

Chapter 21

"Gracias, Señora Sanchez," Braddock said around a mouthful of tortilla and frijoles. When he'd regained consciousness that morning, he wouldn't have given odds on him still being alive by now, let alone eating ravenously. He could feel strength flowing back into him from the food and the strong coffee he sipped between bites.

She still didn't look too happy about him being here, and neither did her husband Enrique. Alphonso and the other six children seemed to find the *Tejano* endlessly fascinating, though. No doubt the Sanchezes had used stories of the Texas devils to frighten their children into behaving, and now here was one of them sitting right in their own jacal. So far he hadn't eaten the head off of any of them.

Sanchez said, "You are certain, señor, that the man who tried to kill you will not come here and harm my family?"

"I don't see how that could ever happen," Braddock said. "I told you, he's convinced I'm dead."

"You cannot *know* this, señor. You cannot be certain of what is in a man's head."

"No, I suppose not, but I'm convinced it's true in this case. You see, this fella...he wouldn't want me on his trail. We didn't know each other for very long, but I reckon he understood that about me. If he didn't believe he'd killed me, he would have kept on looking for me."

Sanchez sighed and said, "It seems all I can do is trust you. I cannot blame my wife for helping you. She has a good heart."

"You have a good family," Braddock said. "If I can ever pay you back for all you've done, I will."

Sanchez glanced at the open door, where the last light of day faded, and said, "Just go, señor, as soon as it is dark, and do not come back here again."

Braddock had slept about half the day, then woken up long enough for Señora Sanchez to clean his wounds again and change the dressings she had put on them after he passed out. While he was awake, Alphonso had fed him some hot stew. Then Braddock had gone back to sleep, and when he woke up in the late afternoon, his fever had broken and he was extremely hungry and thirsty.

Since then he'd had more of the thick stew with chunks of goat meat swimming in it, along with tortillas and beans and a couple of cups of coffee. Señora Sanchez had changed his bandages again, binding them tightly in place with strips of cloth.

"Be careful," she had told him. "Do not move around too much."

That would be difficult, because he had things to do, but he didn't tell her that.

Wouldn't want her to think all her hard work keeping him alive might go to waste before the night was over.

When he'd finished eating, Braddock reclaimed his gun and cleaned and dried it as best he could. It seemed to be in good working order, but he wished he had his gear so he could give it a good cleaning. Everything he owned was back in the boarding house in El Paso, though.

Only about thirty-six hours had passed since his meeting with E.J. Caldwell in the Camino Real. With everything that had happened, it seemed more like weeks to Braddock.

Señora Sanchez shooed the youngsters away from the table while Braddock worked on his gun. Her husband sat on the other side of the table and regarded Braddock gloomily. He had some tequila in one of the clay cups and sipped it now and then.

"What are you going to do?" he asked.

"Well, since you don't have a horse I can buy or rent, and I figure I'd look sort of foolish riding that burro with my feet scraping the ground, I reckon I'll walk back to Juarez. It's not much more than a mile, you said."

"You are shot last night, nearly bleed to death, and now you would walk a mile back into the face of danger. Most people would say you are loco."

Braddock smiled faintly and said, "I've been called that before, and worse." He shook his head. "But what else am I going to do? You don't want me staying here."

"It is true, I do not. This farm provides a living of sorts for us. It cannot support a Texan with your appetite, too."

Braddock laughed, and Sanchez smiled a little, then grew more serious as he went on, "You are the sort of man who cannot turn his back on trouble."

"One of these days I might. But not just yet."

"You will keep on saying that until someday it is too late."

"You could well be right about that."

Braddock had resigned himself to such a fate when he put that bullet-holed Ranger badge in his pocket and started riding the dangerous trails alone. But he would do as much good in the world as he could before fate caught up to him.

Tonight, as he told Sanchez, he planned to head back to Juarez. He wasn't sure yet what he would do once he got there, but Wilcox believed he was dead, Palmer wouldn't know what happened to him, and by now Hernandez might have found out that apparently he'd dropped off the face of the earth. None of them would be looking for him.

He had figure out some way to turn that to his advantage.

Satisfied he'd done the best he could with the Colt, he stood up and slid it back into leather. His movements were a little stiff, partially because he was sore and partially because Señora Sanchez had tied the bandages so tight.

He reached into his pocket and found a couple of silver dollars. One he gave to Señora Sanchez, the other to Alphonso.

"Gracias to both of you," he said. "You saved my life, and I'll never forget it."

"You are leaving now?" Alphonso asked.

"I have to."

"But you will come back to see us someday?"

Braddock glanced at the boy's father, who scowled.

"None of us knows the future, Alphonso, but this I do know: wherever the two of us are from now on, we will be amigos."

The boy's face lit up in a smile.

Sanchez followed Braddock outside, where the last of the daylight was gone and the stars were beginning to come out overhead.

"I would tell you to go with God," the farmer said, "but I think you already have a companion."

"El Diablo?" Braddock said with a grim smile.

"Es verdad," Sanchez said.

Chapter 22

It didn't take long for Braddock to discover he wasn't as well-rested as he'd thought he was. Putting one foot in front of the other required a lot of effort and determination, but he kept doing it anyway.

He followed the river toward the bordertowns on each side of the Rio Grande. After a while he could see their lights ahead of him.

Señora Sanchez had removed his boots and allowed them to dry outside in the sun during the day, but even so, they still weren't made for walking. Braddock paused, leaned against a mesquite, and pulled them off so he could walk in his stocking feet. He had spent a lot of his life on horseback, so being a-foot rubbed him the wrong way.

Maybe he should have considering borrowing that burro from the Sanchezes after all...

He didn't know how long it took him to cover the mile or so to Juarez. An hour, maybe, although it seemed longer. When he reached the outskirts of town he stopped and put his boots on again, then headed for Hernandez's place without any clear plan in mind, thinking only that whatever he did next, Hernandez's was a place to start.

The long walk had given him time to think about everything he had learned the night before. The women and girls who had been kidnapped from Santa Rosalia were the key to the whole affair, he decided. Shadrach Palmer had whores upstairs at Casa de Palmer, and if the rumors about his extensive criminal connections were true, he probably had a piece of every brothel in El Paso. He would need a steady supply of women.

Maybe Hernandez, in partnership with the bandit Martin Larrizo, had an arrangement with Palmer to supply those women, in exchange for the shipment of army rifles. Those Krags were worth more than the prisoners Carmen had told Braddock about. That was a callous thing to think, Braddock knew, but it was true. However, those unfortunates might be just the first installment on the payment.

There were plenty of other villages Larrizo, Gonsalvo, and the other bandits could raid.

Braddock wasn't sure why they wanted the rifles, other than the fact outlaws always wanted more and better weapons. Maybe Larrizo harbored some crackpot notion of staging a revolution and setting himself up as dictator of this part of Mexico. Loco schemes like that were common south of the border. Every common bandido fancied himself an emperor, it seemed.

That idea had begun to form in his mind after Carmen had told him about the captives, and after turning the theory over and over in his head during the walk to Juarez, it seemed even more reasonable and likely.

If Braddock had made the correct assumption, hundreds of women, maybe more, eventually would face an ugly fate. And untold numbers of innocent men, women, and children might die if Larrizo managed to rally an army, even a small one, and launch a revolution. The effort might be doomed to failure, but it would be a bloody slaughter while it lasted.

Braddock had no proof of the plotters' intentions, but his instincts told him he was right.

Even if he wasn't, those women were still being held captive somewhere not far from Juarez. He had to find them and help them somehow.

All those thoughts led him to Hernandez's place, where he circled around to the rear of the big, brightly lit building.

He had in mind seeing if there was a back door so he slip inside and maybe reach the second floor without being seen. He wanted to talk to Carmen again and try to find out more from her about where the prisoners were being held.

A stable stood behind the building, and as soon as Braddock saw it he thought about saddling a horse and tying it somewhere nearby, in case he had to make a quick getaway. Before he could even attempt that, however, the question of whether Hernandez's place had a back door was answered. Light slanted out toward the stable from the door as it swung open.

Braddock pulled back in the shadows beside the stable.

Four men walked out of the building and came toward the stable. Braddock eased an eye around the corner to take a look at them.

Hernandez strode along a few feet in front of the other three. Tonight he wore black trousers, a short black charro jacket, and a flat-crowned black hat.

The other three were dressed like vaqueros in rough clothing and sombreros, but the guns they wore told Braddock they were pistoleros, not cowboys. Hernandez's bodyguards, more than likely.

Clearly, Hernandez intended on going somewhere, as he had the previous evening. Braddock wondered where.

One possible answer suggested itself to him immediately.

Braddock heard Hernandez say something about "the mission" as the men went into the stable. He didn't know if Hernandez meant the errand that brought them out tonight or a specific place, a Catholic mission. Plenty of those could be found all over the region.

Braddock could tell from the noises within the stable that the men were saddling horses. A harsh voice, instantly recognizable as not being Hernandez's smooth tones, said, "Something is wrong with my cinch. The buckle is coming loose."

"Fix it and catch up to us," Hernandez snapped. A moment later, he rode out with the other two men. They turned south.

Braddock stood tensely in the shadows. With Hernandez and some of his men gone, he stood a better chance of being able to sneak into the main building without being discovered.

But another opportunity had presented itself, and Braddock didn't want to waste it. The chance might not amount to anything, but there was only one way to find out.

Hernandez and the other two men had ridden out of sight by the time the third man emerged from the stable.

Braddock was waiting for him, gun in hand.

The pistolero wasn't expecting any trouble, right here behind his boss's headquarters. He rode loosely in the saddle. The horse had taken only a few steps when Braddock dashed out of his hiding place. He grabbed the man's arm and jerked him out of the saddle violently enough that the man's sombrero flew off. Braddock struck swiftly with the Colt, which he had reversed in his hand.

The gun butt thudded hard against the pistolero's skull. The man grunted and tried feebly to struggle. Braddock hit him again.

This time the pistolero went limp.

Braddock holstered the Colt and reached down to take hold of the unconscious gunman under the arms. He dragged the man into the stable, which was dimly lit by a lantern hanging on a nail in one of the posts holding up the roof. Braddock spied a pile of straw and dumped the pistolero on it.

The man's breathing was shallow. He might wake up after a while, or he might not. Knowing the pistolero worked for Hernandez and probably had plenty of blood on his hands, Braddock didn't really care either way. He found a pitchfork and heaped straw over the man until it completely covered the senseless form.

Using the pitchfork made Braddock think of Señora Sanchez. He checked the bandages she had placed on his injuries. Neither of them felt wet, so maybe his exertions hadn't started the wounds bleeding again.

What he hoped he would discover when he followed Hernandez and the other two men made him not mind running the risk of re-opening the wounds.

The horse had danced off a few yards when Braddock grabbed its rider, but it still stood in front of the stable. Braddock approached slowly and carefully, talking in a low voice. Horses had always responded well to him, and this one was no exception. The animal let him get hold of the reins.

A thought occurred to Braddock. Before swinging up into the saddle, he looked around and found the pistolero's sombrero lying on the ground nearby. He picked it up and put it on. That would make him look less suspicious to anyone who saw him.

Then, with a grim smile on his face, he mounted up and rode after his quarry.

Chapter 23

Braddock knew only one main road led out of Juarez heading south, but he didn't know whether or not Hernandez and the others planned to take it. So he pushed the pistolero's horse at a fairly rapid pace starting out. The men had about a ten minute lead on him, but he thought he could make that up.

He had to be careful, though, because he didn't want to ride right up behind them and have them spot him. Even though he rode the third man's horse and wore his hat, he knew he couldn't maintain the masquerade more than a few seconds. It was a fine line, getting close enough to spot them without being spotted himself.

No doubt Hernandez would wonder what had happened to his third bodyguard, but Braddock didn't believe the man would turn back from his errand because of that.

He hadn't seen any sign of the men he was after by the time he reached the edge of town. Braddock reined in for a moment and let out an exasperated sigh. All he could do was keep going on the main road, he decided.

A few minutes later, he came up behind an old, white-bearded peon slowly pulling a handcart. The man must have taken produce or maybe some chickens into Juarez to the market and was late getting started back to his farm. Braddock pulled up beside him and said with the sort of harsh arrogance he figured the pistolero would have used, "Hey, viejo, did three men ride this way a little while ago?"

The old-timer nodded and said, "Sí, señor. They rode very fast. I had to pull my cart aside, else they would have trampled me."

"That's what you get for being in the way." Braddock started to ride on, then paused and added, "But gracias for your help."

"De nada, señor."

Braddock didn't have any more silver dollars, but he had a fifty-cent piece, he recalled. He found it and tossed to the old man, who displayed good reflexes despite his age by catching it in the dim moonlight.

Braddock rode on. Hernandez and his men had been in a hurry, according to the old-timer, but whether or not that actually meant anything was open to question. Hernandez might easily be the sort of man who always charged ahead aggressively, no matter what, and to hell with anybody who got in his way. Braddock could believe that, even though he had met the man only briefly.

He stopped occasionally to listen, and finally he heard the swift rataplan of hoofbeats ahead of him. Several horses, judging by the sound. Braddock had a strong hunch he had found the men he was looking for.

But then the next time he stopped, he didn't hear anything. Either Hernandez and his men had increased their speed and gotten out of earshot again...

Or else they had reached their destination and halted.

Braddock reined his mount to a slower speed. His keen eyes scanned the shadowed landscape ahead of him.

There wasn't much out here in this semi-desert region. An occasional jacal, dark because the peons who lived there were asleep after a hard day of trying to scratch a living out of the land they worked. Clumps of scrubby mesquite trees and stretches of chaparral. Low but rugged mountains looming darkly in the distance like a great, slumbering beast.

And something else squatted a couple of hundred yards off to the left of the road, an irregular pattern of light and shadow against the gray, sandy terrain.

It was a structure of some sort, Braddock realized, but it wasn't all still standing. The roof was gone, and the walls had partially collapsed. The ruins of some old building.

An abandoned mission, maybe, with an intact cellar suitable for holding captives?

A minute later, Braddock came to a trail that branched off from the main road and led toward the ruins. He rode on past it without slowing. Hernandez might have a man watching the trail.

It wasn't likely he would have a man watching the back of the place, though. Not this far from town, in such an isolated area.

Braddock rode another half-mile before leaving the road. He struck out across the country, looping wide around the ruins, and finally reined in. He swung down from the saddle and tied the horse's reins to a mesquite.

From there he went ahead on foot, and after a few minutes he spotted the ruins again. As he worked his way closer, he saw he was right about how the roof and portions of the walls had fallen in. Looming higher at one end of the old building stood the remains of a bell tower. They looked sturdy enough to support a man, and if Hernandez was smart, he'd have a rifleman up there watching the trail from the road.

Braddock crouched in the chaparral and kept an eye on the place for long minutes. Finally he saw the flare of a match in the tower's remnants. Somebody was up there, all right, and had just lit a cigarette.

Braddock could only hope they weren't looking in his direction as he began to creep closer. As much as possible, he stuck to the shadows cast by clumps of mesquite.

Off to one side of the old mission stood a hitch rack with three saddled horses tied to it. On the other side of the mission, a corral held several more horses. Braddock would have been willing to bet Hernandez's men had had to repair the corral before they could use it, maybe even just about rebuild it.

Everything he saw told him he had come to the right place. Hernandez and the two pistoleros had ridden out here from Juarez, and several more men had been here to start with. Maybe the guards were changing shifts. Maybe Hernandez liked to come and check on the prisoners every night. After all, they meant a great deal to him.

If Braddock was right, they represented partial payment for that shipment of Krags.

He hunkered there, ignoring the dull ache in his wounded side, for long minutes. At last three men emerged from the ruins and went to the horses tied at the hitch rack. One of them was Hernandez; Braddock could tell that from his hat. He didn't know if the others were the men who had accompanied

Hernandez from Juarez or two of the men who had already been here at the mission, and it didn't really matter. All three mounted up and rode off into the night.

That left approximately four men at the old mission—and an outlaw Ranger lurking outside, wondering if those kidnapped women were really here.

He didn't intend to leave until he had the answer.

Chapter 24

Braddock focused his attention on the bell tower. If anyone was going to discover him as he approached, likely it would be the guard posted there.

Braddock's eyes had adjusted to the darkness, so after a while he was able to tell the guard had a routine of sorts. He spent most of his time watching the trail from the main road, but every few minutes he turned in a complete circle, pausing at each compass point to study the surrounding countryside in that direction.

Braddock waited until the guard had just finished that survey before he left the thick shadow where he crouched and quickly catfooted forward. He knew he ought to have several minutes before the guard swung around in his direction again.

He covered half the distance to the ruined mission before he went to ground again in the gloom of another mesquite thicket. He might have had time to reach the nearest wall, but he didn't want to risk it.

Patiently, he waited for the guard to make another turn. That gave him a chance to spot a small, flickering orange glow somewhere inside the mission. Not surprisingly, Hernandez's other men had built a campfire in there. Enough of the half-fallen walls still stood upright to keep it from being noticed from the road, and the flames would provide warmth. It got chilly out here on the desert at night, even in the middle of summer.

So Braddock knew where to look for the other men as he slipped up to the crumbling wall a few minutes later. When he listened closely, he could hear the voices of two of them talking quietly to each other.

Like most men, they were complaining about their boss.

"—never know the difference. Hernandez has one of them.

Why should we be deprived of the pleasures due us as men?"

"Because he pays our wages, and because if he feels like it, he can have us strung up and lashed within an inch of our lives, and there is not one damned thing we can do about it. Besides, he didn't have Gonsalvo bring him that girl for his own use. Gonsalvo said Hernandez wanted to put her to work in his place, to see what kind of whores we had brought him."

Braddock knew they were talking about Carmen. The comments jibed with what she had told him about her experiences.

"It's still not fair," the first man said. "Larrizo had her all the way here, now Hernandez—or his customers—have her, and you and I, we have nothing, amigo."

"Nothing but the promise of an easy life when Martin is the president, you mean."

The first man snorted. "A promise is like the call of a night bird. Here and then gone, nothing but a pleasant memory that actually accomplishes nothing."

A third voice spoke up, saying, "Will you two bastards shut up so I can sleep?"

"Bernardo, you cannot think it is fair for us to be around all those women, yet never are we allowed to touch them."

"When you get to be my age, you dung beetle, women matter very little except for what they can cook."

Both the other men laughed, and one said, "I hope I never get to be as old as you, Bernando."

"It is doubtful you will."

Crouched in the darkness on the other side of the wall, Braddock smiled.

He intended to see to it that none of these men got any older than they already were tonight.

With maybe one exception, he corrected himself as an idea sparked in his mind.

He moved carefully along the wall until he reached a spot where nearly all of it had collapsed. Taking off the sombrero, he eased his head around the ragged edge so he could look toward the fire.

The two men who had been talking sat beside the fire,

warming themselves. The third man, Bernardo, stretched out a few yards away in a bedroll. He represented the least threat because it would take him longer to get out of those entangling blankets.

Braddock eyed the Winchesters leaning against a large chunk of adobe that had toppled into the mission at some point. He carried only his Colt and the spare cartridges in his shell belt. While he believed the revolver would work after he had cleaned it at the Sanchez farm, he would feel better about things if he could get his hands on one of those repeaters and maybe the bandolier of ammunition worn by one of the guards.

Braddock pulled back a little and felt around on the ground until he found a chunk of broken adobe slightly bigger than his hand. He drew back his arm and heaved the chunk in a high arc that carried it across what had been the sanctuary to the other side of the mission. It thudded, bounced, thudded again.

Almost instantly, the two men leaped to their feet with their guns drawn. They wheeled around to face the source of the sound.

"Bernardo!" one of them said in an urgent whisper. "We heard something."

"Well, go see what it was," Bernardo said without getting up. Evidently he was in charge of this guard detail. "Probably just a coyote."

The men left the rifles leaning against the chunk of fallen wall and stalked toward the far side of the mission. They thrust their revolvers out in front of them in a stiff, tense manner, obviously ready to start firing at the least excuse.

Braddock swung his leg over the collapsed wall and stepped into the old mission. Bernardo had his head tucked down with the brim of his sombrero shielding him from the glare of the fire. When Braddock got close enough, the man would be able to see him, but with any luck it would be too late to make a difference.

Only a few feet separated Braddock from the rifles when Bernardo suddenly shifted, muttered, lifted his head, and then ripped out a curse.

"Over here!" the older guard cried as he started trying to throw the blankets aside so he could claw for his gun. "Over here!"

Chapter 25

Braddock's Colt roared as he shot one of the guards on the other side of the mission. The bullet caught the man in the side as he tried to turn around. He staggered and fell as bloody froth from his punctured lungs spewed from his lips.

"Felipe!" Bernardo shouted. "Felipe, down here!"

So Felipe was the one in the tower. Braddock would get to him in due time—if Felipe didn't get to him first.

But in the meantime, Braddock fired a round over the head of the second guard across the mission, then turned and shouted toward the front of the ruins, "Wilcox! Get the man in the tower!"

The second guard had ducked away from Braddock's shot and now scrambled for cover behind the collapsed wall on the other side. Braddock's next bullet kicked up dirt at his feet an instant before he flung himself over the wall.

As Braddock pivoted, he saw he had almost neglected Bernardo for too long. The man had gotten untangled from his bedroll and started to raise his gun. Firelight glinted off the weapon's barrel and threw a red glare across the man's angular, gray-bearded face.

Braddock's gun roared a fraction of a second before Bernardo's, but that served to throw off the guard's aim as Braddock's slug tore into his chest. Braddock felt the heat of Bernardo's bullet as it skimmed beside his cheek without touching it.

Bernardo gasped and fell back, but he didn't drop his gun until Braddock shot him again.

The sombrero flew off Braddock's head as a rifle cracked from the bell tower. Braddock dived over the big chunk of adobe where the rifles leaned and snagged the barrel of one of the Winchesters. He rolled onto his belly and saw a muzzle flash from the other side of the mission where the second guard had taken cover.

Braddock returned that fire, cranking off three rounds as fast as he could work the rifle's lever. The bullets struck the top of the ruined wall and sprayed chips of adobe in the second guard's face. He cried out as he fell back.

The rifle in the tower continued to crack, but the piece of fallen wall protected Braddock. He crawled along on his belly until he reached a spot where he could thrust the Winchester's barrel around the stone and line up a shot.

He and Felipe must have spotted each other at the same instant, because the man in the tower swung his rifle and fired just as Braddock squeezed the Winchester's trigger. The sharp reports blended together and sounded like one instead of two.

Felipe's bullet whined off the adobe a few inches from Braddock, while the outlaw Ranger's shot made Felipe lurch upright on the part of the tower's wooden platform that remained intact. Hunched over against the pain, he stumbled forward a step and dropped the rifle.

A second later, he pitched off thc platform, turned over once in the air, and smashed down on his back on the ground just inside the mission.

"You got him, Dex!" Braddock yelled. "There's just one of them left. He can't stop all of us from getting those women."

Braddock sprayed four more rounds toward the guard who had taken cover on the far side of the mission. No shots came in return this time.

Instead, as Braddock lowered the rifle and listened, he heard hoofbeats pounding on the desert floor, heading away from the mission. A bleak grin curved his lips.

He waited five minutes after the sound of the hoofbeats faded out before moving from cover, just to make sure the guard wasn't trying anything tricky. When he was convinced the man had fled, he stood up and moved quickly away from the fire, back into the shadows along the ruined wall. His dangerous life had ingrained such caution in him.

Braddock let a few more minutes go by, then went in search of the entrance to the mission's cellar.

The elements had taken their toll on the adobe walls of the mission. It might have been a hundred years or more since the priests had abandoned it. But the stone and mortar and thick wooden beams that formed the cellar could still be intact.

After a few minutes, set against what had been one of the mission's rear walls, Braddock found a heavy wooden door set into the ground at a slant. It looked fairly new and was barred from the outside. Somebody—Hernandez or one of his men, more than likely—had found this old mission, discovered the cellar was still usable, and decided it would make a good place to store contraband.

There was no better way to describe the women and girls who had been kidnapped from Santa Rosalia, at least where Hernandez, Larrizo, and Shadrach Palmer were concerned. Those captives were a commodity to be traded, nothing more.

That thought made anger smolder inside Braddock. He set the rifle aside, removed the bar from the door, and then grasped its handle. With a grunt of effort, he swung it up and to the side. Its hinges creaked from the sand that had gotten into them.

Then he picked up the rifle, stepped back, and called in Spanish, "You can all come out now. You're safe."

Chapter 26

It took a couple of minutes before one of the captives gathered enough courage to stick her head up into the silvery light from the moon and stars. That glow shone on her long, sleek dark hair.

"Señor...?" she said.

Without the sombrero, it was more easily discernible that Braddock was a gringo, not one of the guards who worked for Hernandez and Larrizo. He said again, "You're safe now. Nobody's going to hurt you. Those other men are either dead or gone. You must have heard the shooting, even down there."

The young woman swallowed and nodded. "Sí, señor. We did not know what was happening. We were frightened that someone had come to kill us."

"No. I'm getting you out of here. You're free to go."

"Go, señor?" she repeated. "Go where?"

Well, now, that was a problem, Braddock realized. He had been concerned with rescuing the prisoners and at the same time making it seem as if Shadrach Palmer were double-crossing Hernandez and Larrizo and had sent his men to steal the captives away. That was why Braddock had been happy to let the other guard flee.

Probably the man had almost reached Juarez by now, carrying the news of Palmer's betrayal to Hernandez.

Braddock needed to move quickly himself, but he couldn't just ride off and leave the women to fend for themselves.

"We'll find a place for you," he said. "Right now you need to go back down into the cellar, talk to the others, and tell them we have to get out of here right away."

"They will be frightened..."

Braddock didn't have time for this, but he didn't really have a choice, either.

"You have to convince them. Otherwise it may be too late."

The woman nodded again and disappeared back down the stone steps visible inside the cellar entrance.

The delay chafed at Braddock as he waited for her to reappear with the other prisoners. He could hear a vague murmur of voices from the darkened cellar. After everything that had happened to the women, he wouldn't be surprised if some of them believed this was a trick or trap of some sort.

Finally, though, the young woman he had spoken to reappeared. She came up the steps and out into the ruined mission, leading a long line of women and girls, all of them still wearing the nightclothes they'd had on when the raiders took them from their village.

Braddock had been looking around while he waited. Some low hills lay a couple of miles away, splotched with dark stretches that had to be trees and other vegetation.

He pointed to them and told the women, "You can go to those hills and find some place to hide until I come back for you."

"That is far to walk, and some of us are weak," the one who spoke for them said. "Larrizo's men did not feed us well."

"There are three horses in the corral." Braddock pointed. "Take them. The weakest among you can ride, two on each horse if necessary." He nodded toward the sprawled bodies of the three men he had killed. "There are weapons and ammunition. Take them, too, so if anyone tries to hurt you, you can fight."

"And what if you never come back for us, señor? What if you are dead?"

Braddock considered that for a moment. He certainly couldn't rule out the possibility of his luck finally running out.

"The Rio Grande is north of here," he said, pointing again. "There are farms on both sides of it where good people will take you in and help you return to your home. I would take you there myself, but there are other things I have to do tonight."

"More killing?" the young woman said.

"More than likely."

One of the older women stepped forward and asked, "Why are you doing these things and risking your life for us, señor? You are a gringo, are you not?"

"That doesn't matter," Braddock said. "There are bad men on both sides of the river, and it's my job to deal with them."

He reached into the hidden pocket on his gunbelt and brought out the silver star in a silver circle, the emblem of the Texas Rangers. In this poor light, the women might not be able to see the bullet hole in the center of the badge, but they could make out enough detail to recognize what it was. Braddock heard several of them murmuring about Texas devils.

Let them think whatever they wanted about him. It didn't change what he had to do.

"Señor," the young woman said as Braddock put away the badge. "There was one other kept here for a time...a friend of mine...Her name is Carmen."

"I know her," Braddock said with a nod.

"Then you know where she is? They took her, and we all believed we would never see her again."

"I know where she is," Braddock said, "and I plan to set her free before the night's over."

Chapter 27

Thoughts tumbled crazily through Braddock's head during the swift ride back to the border.

Probably the first thing Hernandez would do when the guard reached him with the news of the attack on the mission was to send men galloping back down there to make sure the prisoners actually were gone.

When they returned to Juarez and confirmed that, Hernandez would be livid. He would believe Palmer had discovered where the women and girls were being held, then decided to double-cross him and grab the prisoners without trading the stolen rifles for them. That way Palmer could sell the rifles to someone else and get a new supply of whores, too.

If Braddock's theory about the arrangement between Palmer and Hernandez being an ongoing one was correct, the double-cross idea wouldn't stand up to prolonged scrutiny.

Braddock had a hunch Hernandez might be too furious for any such scrutiny, though. In the heat of the moment, he would want to strike back at the man he believed had betrayed him.

He would go after Palmer.

It had to be tonight, too, if Braddock's plan was going to work. If Hernandez waited until the morning and investigated further around the old mission, he or his men would see the prints Braddock had left and realize there had been only one attacker. Braddock could only hope Hernandez was more impulsive than that.

Instead of riding directly through the middle of Juarez, Braddock circled around the bordertown and swam the horse across the Rio Grande a short distance downstream. He stuck to the back streets as he made his way toward Casa de Palmer.

When he reached the place, he left the horse in the alley

behind the building. He wondered briefly what had happened to the pistolero he had "borrowed" the horse from. He might never know, Braddock thought, so he put the question out of his mind.

A set of rear stairs beckoned him. If he strode openly into the saloon, he might encounter Wilcox, who would surely try to gun him down before he could reach Palmer. Braddock wasn't afraid to match his speed against that of Wilcox, but putting the rest of his plan in motion mattered more than settling any personal grudges.

Palmer probably had guards on the second floor to protect him, although Braddock hadn't seen any on his previous visit. As he started up the stairs, he knew he needed to be careful anyway.

When he reached the landing, he tried the door and found it unlocked. A place like Casa de Palmer just about had to have a discreet way in and out, because some of the patrons wouldn't want to be seen coming and going, especially if they were conducting "upstairs" business. Braddock's right hand hovered over the butt of the Colt while he used his left to open the door. He stepped inside quickly.

A couple of gas lamps in holders on the wall cast a dim light in the rear hallway. The doors along both sides of the corridor were closed, but Braddock couldn't count on them staying that way. Palmer's soiled doves entertained their customers in those rooms.

Some of the women Braddock had freed from the cellar at the old mission would have wound up here, he thought. And those were the lucky ones, the more attractive ones. The less fortunate would have been forced to toil in even worse places.

At the far end, the hall made a ninety-degree turn to the left. Palmer's suite was located in the front part of the building in that far corner, Braddock recalled, somewhat isolated from the whores' section.

Braddock walked quickly along the corridor, his steps muffled by the carpet runner. If any of the doors opened, he would just keep his head down and move on, as if he'd concluded any business he had up here and was on his way back downstairs for a drink or a hand or two of poker before calling it a night.

No one emerged from any of the rooms during the thirty seconds or so it took him to walk to the other end of the hall. He heard noises coming from behind some of those doors, but nothing out of the ordinary.

When he reached the corner, he paused to take a look around it. There was the door to Palmer's suite he remembered, no more than forty feet away from him.

But between Braddock and the suite, a tough-looking hombre sat in a ladderback chair with his right ankle cocked on his left knee as he smoked a quirley. The only reason for him to be there was to guard the entrance to the suite.

He looked fully capable of doing that, too, with broad shoulders, a slab of a beard-stubbled jaw, a long-barreled, .44-caliber Remington holstered on his hip, and a double-barreled shotgun leaning against the wall beside him.

Braddock didn't recall seeing the man during his visit to Casa de Palmer the previous night, so there was a good chance the man hadn't seen him, either, and wouldn't recognize him. Braddock could approach him, pretending to be a customer returning from one of the whores' rooms. The question was whether the guard would realize he hadn't seen Braddock come upstairs and go around the corner with any of the soiled doves. Braddock had no way of knowing how long the man had been sitting there at his post or how good his memory was, but it was a definite potential risk.

A risk, Braddock knew, that had to be run, because he had to reach Shadrach Palmer before all hell broke loose.

He put the sort of leering grin on his face that a man would wear after a successful visit to the second floor of Casa de Palmer and ambled around the corner, turning toward the guard. The man sat up straighter and moved a hand toward the Greener as he regarded Braddock with a narrow-eyed gaze.

Braddock just grinned even bigger and stupider at him.

The guard grunted and seemed to relax. He didn't pick up the shotgun. Braddock kept moving and gave the man a friendly nod.

"Howdy," he said.

The guard started to say something, probably a return

greeting, but then his eyes abruptly narrowed again. Braddock saw suspicion spring to life in them.

Too late. Braddock had come within reach, and his fist shot out in a powerful blow that landed on the guard's jaw.

It felt about like punching a slab of rock, but it jerked the guard's head to the side and knocked him off the chair. As he went down, Braddock leaped closer, pulled out his Colt, and slammed it against the guard's head to finish the job of knocking him out.

The brief scuffle had made a little noise, but maybe not enough to be heard in Palmer's suite. Braddock couldn't leave the man lying there to be discovered and cause a commotion, so he pouched his iron, stooped, got hold of the senseless guard under the arms, and hauled him upright.

Pain jabbed into Braddock's side where the bullet from Wilcox's derringer had ripped through him twenty-four hours earlier. The wounds were probably bleeding again, but there was nothing Braddock could do about that now.

One way or another, this would be over tonight, he thought, and he could gct some proper medical attention then—if he was still alive to need it.

He propped the guard up and held him with one arm while he used his other hand to twist the doorknob. It turned, and he shoved open the door to Palmer's suite. Braddock lurched through the entrance, taking the guard with him, and then dumped the man on the thick rug on the sitting room floor as he heeled the door shut behind him. His right hand dropped to the gun and slid it from the holster in case Wilcox was in here.

The room had only one occupant, though, and she gasped as she shrank back agains the divan cushions. The silk dressing gown she wore hung open almost to the waist, revealing a lot of smooth, curving, swelling flesh.

"George?" Palmer's mistress Elise said as she stared at him. "What in the world are you doing here?"

Then her rich brown eyes widened even more as she stared down the barrel of Braddock's Colt.

Chapter 28

"Where's Palmer?" Braddock asked, his voice sharp.

"George, I...I don't understand. Dex Wilcox said you disappeared, that something must have happened to you—"

"Is Palmer here?"

"No, he...he's downstairs, I think..."

Two glasses, each with a little bit of wine in it, sat on a small table next to the divan. Braddock glanced at them, then asked, "Is Wilcox in the bedroom?"

"What?" Elise's eyes widened even more. "You think Wilcox and I...how dare you! I would never betray Shad like that. What makes you think I would?"

"There are two glasses."

"Left from when Shad and I had drinks earlier."

He couldn't tell if she lied. He never had been able to read women as well as he could men. He motioned with the revolver's barrel and said, "Go over there and open that door."

She glared at him for a second, then pouted. "I won't. You've insulted me."

"I can knock you out like him—" Braddock nodded toward the unconscious man on the floor. "—and then go see for myself, if that's what you want."

"You wouldn't," she said, her voice as frigid as a blue norther.

He probably wouldn't, Braddock realized, but he didn't say anything and kept his face hard as stone.

After a few more seconds, Elise blew out an exasperated breath and said, "All right. If I have to show you before you'll believe me..."

She stood up, not being too careful about it so the dressing gown gaped even more, and went over to the bedroom door. She threw it open and stepped back, waving a hand to indicate

Braddock should take a look.

"You first," he told her.

Elise walked into the room, turned around to face him, and spread her arms. Braddock ignored all the charms on display and stepped through the door, checking to right and left.

The two of them were the bedroom's only occupants. Braddock stepped over to a large wardrobe and opened it, saw only clothes.

"Are you going to look under the bed like the cuckolded husband in some melodrama?" Elise asked.

"Should I?"

She made that exasperated sound again and pulled the duvet up around the bed. Braddock could see under it without having to bend over.

"Are you satisfied now?"

"I reckon. When do you expect Palmer back up here?"

"I have no idea. He owns this place. He comes and goes as he pleases."

"And he owns you, too, I suppose."

Braddock wasn't sure why he said that. Maybe he just wanted to put a burr under her saddle because of her attitude.

"No one owns me," Elise said in a low, menacing voice. "Least of all Shadrach Palmer. I'm here for my own benefit, not his."

"All right," Braddock said. "I suppose since we're clear about everything, we can talk civilly now. Did you hear the conversation when Palmer talked to Wilcox last night, after Wilcox got back from Juarez?"

"Why should I tell you anything?"

Braddock figured he would get farther by appealing to her mercenary instincts, rather than any other approach, so he said, "Because Palmer's in trouble, he just doesn't know it yet."

"Shad is in danger?"

"He could well be." Braddock told the truth as far as it went, although Braddock himself represented the biggest danger to Palmer right now.

Elise studied him for a moment longer, then pulled the gown closed and tightened the belt around her waist.

"Wilcox came up here to talk to Shad. He told Shad how you killed Larkin and he killed Larkin's two men."

"Wilcox said he killed Larkin's men."

"That's right."

Braddock let that pass. Wilcox had figured he could get away with claiming credit for those two shootings, because he wasn't expecting Braddock to show up again. But it didn't really matter.

"What else?"

"He said you wanted to stop at another cantina and told him to come on back and tell Shad what happened. He claimed you said you'd be along later. So Wilcox did what you asked. Only you never showed up today. Shad sent Wilcox back to the other cantina, and the people there claimed they had never seen you. Shad was upset when Wilcox told him, but Wilcox said you must have been jumped and robbed. He said you might be lying dead in an alley or floating in the Rio Grande." Elise shrugged. "It happens all the time in Juarez."

"So he thinks he got away with it," Braddock murmured.

"Got away with what?" Elise asked.

Braddock stiffened as he heard the sound of a gun being cocked behind him, and then Shadrach Palmer said, "That's what I'd like to know. What are *you* trying to get away with, George?"

Chapter 29

Braddock cursed himself silently for not hearing Palmer come into the room. He had been concentrating on what Elise told him, and Palmer must have been quiet about it. If he had come along and seen the guard missing from the hall outside the suite, that would have made him suspicious.

The situation was even worse than that, Braddock saw as he looked over his shoulder.

Dex Wilcox stood a little behind and to one side of Palmer, a scowl on his face and his hand on the butt of his gun. Both men had stopped just inside the door of the sitting room.

Palmer gestured with the little pistol in his hand. He no longer looked like a shopkeeper. His eyes reminded Braddock more than ever of a rattlesnake, and so did the attitude of his body, poised and ready to strike and kill.

"Back out of there," Palmer went on. "Don't try anything or I'll put a bullet in you."

Braddock backed out of the bedroom. Elise folded her arms and sauntered after him, a smirk on her face now.

And yet concern still lurked in her eyes. Braddock had said something threatened Palmer, and he represented her livelihood right now. She wanted to know more, Braddock thought, so she could protect herself.

"Elise, take his gun," Palmer ordered.

She hesitated, clearly not wanting to get that close to Braddock. A faint smile touched his lips as he told her, "Don't worry. I won't hurt you."

"Damn right you won't hurt her," Palmer said. "If you did, I'd make sure you took a long, painful time to die."

She stepped up to Braddock, licked her lips slightly, and reached out with a slender, long-fingered hand to slide the Colt from its holster. Then she stepped back quickly.

"All right, George, turn around."

"Something's bad wrong here, boss," Wilcox said. "He must figure on tryin' some sort of double-cross. Why else would he drop out of sight like that, then sneak in here, knock out Carson, and force Miss Elise into your bedroom?"

Wilcox talked fast. He wanted to solidify Palmer's suspicions and make sure he considered Braddock guilty of something. Braddock knew that. He just kept a cool, confident smile on his face. It might madden Wilcox into saying too much.

When Palmer didn't respond, Wilcox went on, "Let me take him outta here and deal with him. No need for you to worry yourself about this, Mr. Palmer."

"Wait just a minute," Palmer said as he lifted his free hand. The gun in his other hand remained steady as a rock as he pointed it at Braddock. "I asked George for an explanation, and I'm going to give him a chance to answer me."

"Wilcox is right about a double-cross," Braddock said, "only he's the one trying to pull it."

Wilcox's scowl darkened. He had moved aside so he had a clear shot at Braddock. He started to draw his gun as he snarled, "You damn liar—"

"Dex!" Palmer's sharp tone made Wilcox pause with the gun halfway out of its holster. "I have this under control."

"Sure, boss." With obvious reluctance, Wilcox let his revolver slide back down into leather, but he didn't move his hand far from it.

"Keep talking, George. And remember...this is the only chance to tell the truth you're going to get."

"I don't blame you for being leery of me, Mr. Palmer," Braddock said. "After all, you barely know me. But I did what you said last night. I went to Hernandez's place and killed that fella Larkin."

"And then dropped out of sight," Palmer said, nodded. "I know about Larkin. I want to know what else you were doing."

"Trying not to die after Wilcox shot me. That kept me pretty busy."

Wilcox said, "That's a damn dirty lie!"

"If you'll let me pull up my shirt, I can prove it," Braddock said.

Wilcox started to say something else. Palmer motioned him to silence, thought for a moment about what Braddock had said, then told him, "All right, go ahead, but slow and easy. No tricks."

"No tricks," Braddock agreed. He lifted his shirt to reveal the bandages on his side. "Wilcox wounded me with a little derringer he carries. He'd already tried to smash my head in and drop me in the river to drown."

"Why the hell would I do that?" Wilcox demanded.

"So I wouldn't tell Mr. Palmer how you and Hernandez are planning to steal those army rifles for yourselves, so Hernandez won't have to turn over the women from Santa Rosalia."

Palmer's eyes widened, and so did Wilcox's. Braddock could feel Elise staring at him as well. But after a moment the canny look came back into Palmer's gaze, replacing the surprise, and he said, "Just because someone shot you doesn't mean Dex did it."

"No, but how would I know those things I just told you if I hadn't heard him and Hernandez plotting together? Hell, I just rode into El Paso a couple of days ago!"

"He's loco, boss," Wilcox insisted. "Either that, or he's lyin' to save his own hide since you caught him in here with Elise."

"Wait just a minute," she said coldly. "You had better not be accusing me of anything."

"No, no," Palmer said, waving the idea off as ridiculous. "We all know you'd never do anything to risk your comfortable life, my dear." He turned his attention back to Braddock. "Just what else do you claim to have overheard?"

"Boss, you're not gonna listen to this lyin' son of a bitch, are you?" Wilcox protested.

Palmer ignored him and looked steadily at Braddock, waiting for an answer.

"Wilcox told Hernandez where you've got the rifles stashed, and Hernandez told Wilcox about the old mission south of Juarez where the women are being kept. Hernandez is sending two groups of men across the river tonight. One group will go after the rifles. The other will come here and kill you so Wilcox can take over your operation. That's the other part of their deal."

"By God, that's all I'm gonna take!" Wilcox yelled. He started again to claw at his gun, but Palmer swung around sharply and leveled the pistol at him.

"Stop it, Dex!"

Wilcox stared at him. "Boss—"

"I don't see how George could know everything that's going on unless he's telling the truth," Palmer said. "He knows about the rifles in the warehouse, he knows about the deal with Hernandez...Hell, he even knows where the prisoners are, and that's something Hernandez never told me! He must have told you, though."

Wilcox shook his head. "It's all a pack of lies."

"There's one way to sort it out. Gather up all the men you can, and we'll go to the warehouse and make sure those Krags are safe. If they are—"

Before Palmer could go on, gunfire suddenly roared downstairs. Pistols cracked and a shotgun boomed and women began to scream. It sounded like a war had broken out with no warning.

And so it had.

Chapter 30

Braddock had hoped to stall long enough for Hernandez to make a move. The violent chaos downstairs told him he'd been successful.

Wilcox yanked out his gun. Whether he intended to shoot Braddock or Palmer, Braddock never knew, because Palmer fired before Wilcox could pull the trigger.

Wilcox staggered back, blood welling from the hole in his chest. His revolver had swung wide, but he jerked the trigger in his death spasms and the gun roared.

The slug whipped through the space Elise had occupied a split-second earlier, before Braddock tackled her and knocked her to the floor. Even though Wilcox's knees had buckled, Palmer shot him again, this time in the face. Wilcox went over backward, a red-rimmed hole in the center of his forehead.

Palmer swung around from the dead gunman and said, "Elise! Are you all right?"

Braddock sprawled on top of her, a position that would have been mighty pleasant under other circumstances. He rolled off her so she could sit up, gasping and wide-eyed.

"My God!" she said. "He...he almost *shot* me!"

She had dropped Braddock's gun when he pulled her down. Braddock started to reach for it, then paused and looked back at Palmer.

Palmer jerked his head in a nod and said, "Pick it up. I think Dex showed just whose side he was on when he tried to shoot me."

If Palmer wanted to believe that, Braddock didn't mind at all. He scooped his Colt from the rug and stood up. He could have killed Palmer then, but he needed the man alive.

"Get down there and see what's going on," Palmer said. "We

have to deal with this attack and then stop Hernandez from stealing those rifles."

Braddock gave him an equally curt nod and hurried out of the suite.

So far, so good, he thought as he ran along the balcony toward the stairs. He paused at the landing to survey the scene below.

Gunsmoke hung in the air in thick clouds. Hernandez's men must have come in shooting. Palmer's bartenders and bouncers had returned the fire as the customers scattered, scrambling for cover. Braddock didn't see the bodies of any innocents lying around, but one of the bartenders lay face-down on the hardwood with a pool of blood around his head. The crimson had spread out enough to start dripping off the front of the bar.

Braddock barely had time to take that in before a bullet sizzled past his ear. The pistolero who had fired it crouched behind an overturned table, but he had lifted himself too high when he triggered the shot, giving Braddock a target. Braddock drilled the man through the throat. He flopped backward with blood spurting from the wound.

Some of Hernandez's men knelt on the boardwalk in front of the saloon and fired through busted-out windows. Braddock sent a couple of rounds whistling through one of those windows and saw another shape fall.

Hernandez's men outnumbered Palmer's, though, and Braddock realized they couldn't win this fight. He snapped a shot at another pistolero he caught a glimpse of, then turned and raced back to the suite without waiting to see if his bullet had scored.

"There are too many of them," he reported to Palmer after hurrying into the sitting room. "You need to get out of here while you still can, boss."

The guard Braddock had knocked out earlier had regained consciousness. He sat up, shaking his head groggily, but at the sight of Braddock he growled and started to get up.

Palmer closed a hand on his shoulder to stop him. "Forget it, Carson," he said. "Get downstairs and help hold off Hernandez's men. George, you come with me and Elise. We have to warn the men who are guarding those rifles. Maybe Hernandez hasn't gotten to them yet."

Braddock nodded. He would have suggested the same thing if Palmer hadn't beaten him to it. He knew now the rifles were hidden in a warehouse somewhere in El Paso, but he didn't know its exact location.

"If I'm coming with you, I have to get dressed—" Elise began.

"No time." Palmer grabbed her hand. He still held the pistol in his other hand. "Come on."

Braddock had been thumbing fresh cartridges into his Colt while Palmer talked. He held it ready as he led the way through the rear corridor toward the stairs. Frightened faces belonging to soiled doves and customers peeked out from doors open a few inches. Braddock figured as soon as he and Palmer and Elise were gone, a stampede would follow them down the rear stairs.

When he threw the door open and stepped out onto the landing, he caught a glimpse of two men wearing sombreros on their way up. Each man carried a shotgun, so Braddock couldn't give them time to bring the Greeners into play. He fired three times, flame geysering from the Colt's barrel.

The first two slugs hammered into the chest of the man leading the way up the stairs and knocked him back into his companion. Braddock's third bullet blew that man's jaw off. The pistoleros' legs tangled together, and they both tumbled back down the stairs, leaving splashes of dark blood behind. They landed at the bottom in a welter of dead and dying flesh without firing the shotguns.

Elise screamed, then muffled the sound by clapping both hands over her mouth in horror.

"Get hold of yourself," Palmer snapped. "You knew I'm in a violent business."

"I don't see any more of them," Braddock said. "We'd better move while we can. There are bound to be more of Hernandez's men on the way around here."

He went down the stairs as fast as he could and stepped over the corpses at the bottom. Palmer and Elise followed close behind him. Palmer had his left hand clamped around Elise's arm to help her negotiate the grisly obstacle at the bottom of the stairs. She still wore only the dressing gown and slippers, but that couldn't be helped.

A moment later, the three of them had disappeared into the welcoming darkness of the alley.

Chapter 31

The sound of gunfire continued behind them, but it faded as Palmer took the lead and they wound through the back alleys and side streets of El Paso.

The route actually didn't cover all that much distance, Braddock realized as they came to a large, darkened building beside the Rio Grande.

"This is it?" Braddock said. "The place where the rifles are hidden?"

"That's right." Palmer looked around. "And we've beaten Hernandez here."

Of course they had, Braddock thought, since Hernandez didn't know where Palmer had hidden the rifles. Braddock had just wanted Palmer to think that so he'd lead the way here.

Palmer took a ring of keys from his pocket. Braddock said, "You don't have guards posted here?"

"Of course I do, inside and outside both."

As if to prove that, a couple of dark shapes loomed out of the shadows and turned into a pair of men toting rifles.

"What's going on, boss?" one of them asked.

"Hernandez is trying to double-cross us," Palmer said. "He and some of his men may show up here at any minute. Some of them attacked the saloon a little while ago."

"Son of a bitch!" The guard added hastily, "Sorry, Miss Elise. We thought we heard shots in that direction, boss, but we didn't figure they came from Casa de Palmer. If we had, we would've gone to see what the trouble was."

"No, you did the right thing by staying here," Palmer told the men. "Those rifles will set me up for life before I'm through." He started unlocking the regular-sized door beside the big double entrance. "Stay out here and keep your eyes open. If you see any sign of trouble, come on inside. We'll fort up in there." Palmer laughed. "We have enough rifles and ammunition to hold off an army, after all!"

That was true, Braddock supposed. But rifles still needed people to fire them, and he didn't figure Palmer had more than half a dozen men here.

Even if he was right about that number, he still faced steep odds. He couldn't do anything except forge ahead with his hastily formed plan, though.

Braddock followed Palmer and Elise into the warehouse. They stopped in a small office next to the big, open storage space. Palmer lit a lamp on the desk and went out into the warehouse's main room.

Bales of cotton, large tow sacks full of other goods, and stacks of boxes and crates filled about half the space. As a smuggler, Palmer had to have plenty of contraband on hand and in motion across the border.

Braddock had no trouble spotting the particular crates that interested him, however, fifty of them, all long and rectangular and holding twenty Krag-Jorgensen Springfield rifles apiece. Square ammunition boxes rose in stacks next to the crated rifles.

Three men carrying Winchesters emerged from the shadowy recesses of the warehouse's far corners. They nodded politely to Elise, then one of them asked, "Is there some sort of trouble, Mr. Palmer?"

"Damn right there is. Hernandez is on his way here to steal those Krags from me."

"Well, that dirty, double-crossin' greaser! I always figured you couldn't trust a Mex."

"Dex Wilcox was in on it with him."

That shocked the three guards even more. One of them said, "Dex could be a pretty sorry varmint sometimes, but I never thought he'd sell you out."

"He tried to kill me not long ago, as soon as George here told me about his deal with Hernandez."

The three men looked suspiciously at Braddock. One of them asked, "Who in blazes is this?"

"His name's George. He just went to work for me last night,

and already he's saved our bacon by exposing Wilcox's treachery."

The guard's eyes narrowed even more as he stared at Braddock. Then he said, "You're the hombre who killed Larkin and his boys."

Palmer looked at him sharply. "How did you know that?"

"Because I was there, boss. I wasn't on guard duty last night, so I went across the river to Hernandez's place to see a little chiquita there I like. I watched her dance all evenin', but I saw Dex and this hombre come in, and then they left a little while later, after the trouble with Larkin." The man nodded toward Braddock. "George—if that's his name—went upstairs for a while, but Dex was downstairs drinkin' and joshin' with the whores."

"He didn't talk to Hernandez?"

"He couldn't have. I never laid eyes on Hernandez, but Dex was where I could see him the whole time." The man bared his teeth in a grimace at Braddock. "If you been sayin' Dex was a traitor, it's a damn lie!"

Any plan, no matter how meticulously laid out, could be ruined by something unexpected. As haphazard as Braddock's plan had been, he was a little surprised nothing had gone wrong with it before now.

But now he had reached the end of the trail, so there was only one thing he could do.

He smacked the gun in his hand against the side of Palmer's head, driving the man to his knees, then darted toward the crates holding the rifles as he triggered the Colt at Palmer's guards.

Chapter 32

One of the men doubled over as a slug from Braddock's Colt punched into his guts. The bullet bored on through and smashed his spine, dropping him to the floor like a discarded rag doll.

Another guard dropped his rifle and staggered back as he clutched at a bullet-shattered shoulder.

The third man got his rifle working, though, and hammered shots at Braddock as the outlaw Ranger rolled over the stacked-up crates. The bullets narrowly missed Braddock but chewed splinters from the wood. He felt them sting his hands and face.

As he dropped behind the crates, he heard Palmer yell, "Circle around! Get the bastard!"

Boot soles slapped the floor as the guard still on his feet ran through the shadows in an attempt to flank Braddock. Knowing the man couldn't draw a bead on him at the same time, Braddock came up on one knee and leveled the Colt at Palmer. He pulled the trigger, but Palmer had already dived aside so the bullet missed him.

Elise was just standing there, too stunned by everything that had happened to move. Palmer ducked behind her and looped his left arm around her neck to yank her against him as a human shield. With his other hand, he shoved the pistol under her arm and triggered a couple of rounds toward Braddock.

The hurried shots missed, but Braddock had to hold his fire because Palmer had Elise in front of him.

That situation didn't last very long. Elise realized the danger she was in and tried to writhe free from Palmer's grip. Failing that, she grabbed his arm, forced her head down, and sank her teeth into his flesh.

That loosened his hold on her. Elise slammed an elbow against his chest and knocked him back a step. She dived away from him, out of the line of fire.

Palmer tried a desperate shot, but Braddock's Colt roared a hair ahead of Palmer's little revolver. The impact of the slug smashing into him knocked Palmer all the way around so he faced away from Braddock. He fell to his knees, looked back over his shoulder, and opened his mouth.

Blood poured out of it, and then he slumped forward to land on his face.

The third guard's rifle cracked. Braddock felt the wind-rip of a bullet as it went past his ear. He dived, rolled, and came up just as the guard fired another round. The muzzle flash gave Braddock something to aim at in the gloomy warehouse. The Colt roared and bucked in his hand.

The guard dropped his rifle and stumbled back, gurgling and wheezing. He went to one knee and fought to stay upright and alive as he clawed out the gun on his hip.

Braddock sent the final round in the Colt through the man's brain.

He jammed the empty gun back in its holster, vaulted over the crates, and ran over to the man whose shoulder he had broken with his second shot. The guard had collapsed and started writhing in pain. Braddock snatched up the rifle the man had dropped and put him out of his misery temporarily by knocking him out with a stroke of the Winchester's butt.

Hurried footsteps came toward him again. Braddock swung around and leveled the repeater at the two guards who had rushed in from outside.

The men stopped short, not knowing what was going on. Before they could figure it out, Braddock yelled, "Get out of here! The Rangers are on their way! We've been double-crossed!"

The men stared, clearly uncertain what to do, especially now that they had spotted Palmer's body.

Elise stepped up beside Braddock and said in a voice slightly hoarse from Palmer choking her, "Shad's dead. George is right. It's all gone to hell. Save yourselves."

They knew her as their boss's mistress and didn't see any reason why she would lie to them. Braddock could tell when they made up their minds to light a shuck while they still had the chance.

"Son of a bitch," one man muttered, but that was all either of them said before they got out of there as quickly as they could.

"Thank you," Braddock told Elise when they were alone.

"Is that what you really are?" she said. "A Texas Ranger?"

"Something like that."

If the answer confused her, she didn't bother to show it. Instead she glanced at Palmer's body and her lip curled.

"He didn't give a damn about me."

"Did you really think he did?"

"I didn't think he'd try to get me killed, just to save himself!"

"And that's why you helped me?"

She sighed. "I don't know. Just like I don't know what I'm going to do now. But I'm going to be gone from here before the Rangers show up, I can tell you that."

"Good luck to you, then. And thanks again for your help."

"Maybe I'll see you again sometime, Mr. Something Like a Ranger."

"Maybe," Braddock said, but he didn't really believe it.

Chapter 33

Half an hour later, Braddock knocked softly on the door of Elizabeth Jane Caldwell's room in the Camino Real.

With a bloodstain showing on his side where the bandages had soaked through to his shirt, and his face and hands grimy from powdersmoke, he didn't look like the usual denizen of the fancy hotel. Because of that, he had snuck in through a service entrance and hoped he wouldn't encounter anyone on his way up to the room.

He hadn't. Now he hoped the reporter would answer the door pretty soon, since someone could still come along. He knocked again and said, "Miss Caldwell?"

She opened the door and peered out at him in shock. Her tousled blond hair and the blue robe she had wrapped around her told him she had been in bed.

Well, why wouldn't she be? It was well after midnight, after all. Most self-respecting people were asleep by now, even journalists.

"Mr. Braddock," she said. He could tell she tried not to sound shocked.

"I'm going to make an improper suggestion and ask you to invite me in."

"Wait...you mean...Yes, of course." She stepped back. "Come in." She caught sight of the blood on his shirt. "You're injured!"

"Shot, actually," he said as he stepped inside and she closed the door behind him. "But it happened more than twenty-four hours ago and it hasn't killed me yet, so maybe it won't for a while."

"I...I didn't expect you to get hurt."

"You sent me after people who hold up trains, steal rifles, and wipe out army escorts, not to mention other things just as bad you don't even know about. What the hell did you expect to happen?" Braddock laughed humorlessly. "Never mind. I get cranky when people try to kill me all the time." He held out a key he took from his pocket. "This opens the door of a warehouse down by the river." He told her exactly where to find the place.

She took the key and asked, "What's in there?"

"A thousand Krag-Jorgensen Springfields, and the body of one of the men responsible for stealing them, along with a few of the varmints who worked for him. I dragged one of them who was still alive outside into the alley before I locked the place up, but he may well have bled to death by now."

"Good Lord, you're...you're cold-blooded."

"Just trying to get the job done," Braddock said. "It's possible you and I are the only ones still alive who know the rifles are there...Well, one other person," he added, thinking of Elise, "but I don't reckon you have to worry about that. You've got contacts at Fort Bliss, you said. I know it's the middle of the night, but you'd better get dressed, hire a buggy, and get out there as quick as you can so you can tell them where to find the guns."

"Of course. You can stay here. I'll summon a doctor for your wounds—"

"Not hardly," Braddock said. "Once this is all over, I'll write you a letter and explain everything, but for now, just get those Krags back where they belong."

He turned toward the door, but she caught his sleeve and stopped him.

"I still owe you—"

"Send whatever you think is fair to the mission in Esperanza, where you sent that letter to me. The padre there will put it to good use if I don't get back to claim it. Hell, even if I do, I'll probably give most of it to him anyway."

"Because you don't really work for money, do you?" she asked, her blue eyes peering up at him. "You do what you do—"

"Because it's my job," Braddock said harshly, "and it's not over yet."

Chapter 34

Braddock didn't know how the battle at Casa de Palmer had turned out, but he didn't give in to his curiosity and steered clear of the saloon instead. After a small-scale war like that, the El Paso police had probably swarmed the place, and he was still a wanted man, after all.

Instead he reclaimed his dun from the livery stable, annoying a sleepy hostler. Some of his gear remained at the boarding house where he had barely stayed, but nothing he couldn't live without. This time he rode across the Rio Grande on the bridge he had fallen from a night and a day and most of another night earlier, then headed for Hernandez's place.

Dawn wasn't far off by the time he got there. Establishments like this never really closed, but usually by this time of the morning they had settled down to a pretty drowsy state. Braddock counted on that to help him get what he had come here for.

He left the dun by the stable behind the building and walked toward the rear door. Steel whispered against leather as he drew his gun. The Colt had a full cylinder, and Braddock would use every one of the bullets if he had to.

He was lightheaded again and felt somehow outside of himself. Exhaustion, strain, and loss of blood would do that to a fella, he supposed. But as he had told Elizabeth Jane Caldwell, he hadn't finished the job.

By now, the young woman might have notified the army about the location of the stolen rifles. Braddock knew the warehouse's thick walls had muffled the shots inside it. Anyway, nobody paid much attention to gunshots in that part of town. Those Krags would sit there undisturbed until the proper authorities came for them.

Nobody was going to help Carmen, though, and he had promised the women at the mission he would get her out of here.

Not only that, but Hernandez was still alive, and he was partially responsible for the deadly raid on Santa Rosalia. He had to pay for that.

He would settle up with Martin Larrizo some other time, Braddock told himself. Hell, one man couldn't take on the whole world at the same time, now could he?

The back door of Hernandez's place was locked.

Braddock muttered a curse and fished out his knife. After a few minutes of working the blade at the lock and the jamb, he put his shoulder against the door and pushed. It popped open. He stepped inside and found himself inside a pitch-black room.

After pushing the door up behind him, he fished a lucifer from his pocket and snapped it to life with his thumbnail, squinting against the sudden glare. He was in some sort of storeroom, with crates of empty bottles sitting around. A door on the other side of the room let out into a short hall that ran toward the front of the building.

Close by at Braddock's right hand, stairs rose to the second floor. They would lead just about to where Hernandez's living quarters were located, Braddock recalled.

He went up, staying close to the wall so the steps wouldn't creak as much. When he got to the top, he saw a door he remembered and knew it led into Hernandez's rooms. Braddock closed his hand around the knob and twisted it silently.

He stepped inside quickly, gun up and ready. A lamp on a side table was turned down low, but it cast enough light for him to see Hernandez sprawled in an armchair, legs outstretched, a glass of what was probably tequila in his right hand. He was bare from the waist up and his left arm was wrapped in bandages.

Hernandez stared stupidly at the intruder. Braddock realized the man was drunk. He could have put a bullet in Hernandez right then and there and ended his evil, but that would rouse the rest of the place and wouldn't help Carmen.

"You!" Hernandez said. "Palmer's man! Have you come to betray me, too?"

"Palmer's dead," Braddock said flatly. "I'm nobody's man and never have been. As for why I'm here, I'm taking Carmen."

Hernandez frowned and looked confused for a moment before his expression cleared.

"The little whore from Santa Rosalia?" he said. "She's why you risked your life coming here?"

"That's one reason."

Hernandez must have figured out what Braddock meant. His face clouded. Then, even though he didn't appear to have any weapons, he suddenly flung the glass of tequila at Braddock and launched himself after it in a desperate dive.

The fiery liquor hit Braddock in the face and stung his eyes. He chopped at Hernandez's head with the gun but couldn't stop the man from ramming into him. They both went down with a crash that shook the floor underneath them and jolted the gun out of Braddock's hand.

He swung a fist at Hernandez's head and connected with a glancing blow. Hernandez seemed to have sobered up in a hurry, though, because he shook it off and slammed punches of his own at Braddock. Braddock tried to fend them off, but his head jerked from side to side under the impacts. He knew if Hernandez hit him many more times, he would pass out.

His hands shot up and grabbed Hernandez by the throat. Braddock mustered all the strength he could and rolled over, putting Hernandez underneath him. He hung on for dear life as he dug his thumbs into the man's neck.

Hernandez bucked and thrashed and flailed at him, but Braddock ignored it. He knew if he let go, he was a dead man, so he bore down harder. Hernandez's eyes grew wide and began to bulge out until it seemed they were about to burst from their sockets. His handsome face was ugly now as it turned a deep shade of purple.

Hernandez bucked a couple more times, then a sharp stink reached Braddock's nose. Hernandez's bowels had emptied as death claimed him. The wide, staring eyes began to turn glassy.

Braddock let go. His chest heaved as he tried to catch his breath.

Something crashed into his injured side, filling him with agony until it seemed he would explode. He rolled over, looked up, and through pain-blurred eyes saw a tall, burly man with a heavy black mustache looming over him, ready to kick him again. The man wore only the bottom half of a pair of long underwear, but he looked powerful enough to tear Braddock apart with his bare hands, especially considering the shape the outlaw Ranger was in at the moment.

"You've killed Paco," the man rumbled. Braddock realized he meant Hernandez. "No matter. The revolution will go on, as soon as I find those damned rifle—"

The man stopped short and gasped. He stumbled a step forward, twisted and tried to reach behind him. He couldn't reach whatever he tried to grab. Slowly, he kept twisting around until Braddock saw the handle of what must have been a long, heavy knife protruding from his back.

Then, with a gurgling moan, the man collapsed and died. With him out of the way, Braddock saw Carmen standing there, nude, hair disheveled, bruises and scratches on her face.

"They both took out their anger on me," she said in a voice that trembled slightly. "First Hernandez, then Larrizo. But now they are dead, and I live."

Braddock pushed himself up on an elbow and looked at the man Carmen had stabbed. "That's...Martin Larrizo?"

"Sí. The revolution...is over."

Until some other would-be dictator tried to seize power for himself, Braddock thought, even if it meant the deaths of thousands of innocent people.

He wanted to lie back and rest, but he knew he couldn't. Instead, he struggled to climb to his feet and told Carmen, "Get dressed. I've come to take you out of here. To take you home."

"But you are hurt!"

"I'll make it," he told her. "I'll see that you're safe."

"After all that has happened...how can I ever be safe again?"

Braddock didn't have an answer for that. Time would heal Carmen, or it wouldn't. He had done all he could.

At least, he would have once he had delivered her and the other women back to Santa Rosalia.

"We've got to go," he said. "I don't know if anybody else heard that commotion, but we can't risk it."

She swallowed and nodded. "You are sure you can make it?"

Braddock wasn't sure of anything, but he put a smile on his face and said, "Let's go home."

Chapter 35

Braddock moved one of the knights on the chessboard and said, "Check."

The padre moved his king out of danger for the moment. Braddock slid a rook across the board to close in on his royal prey, and his opponent angled a bishop into position and said, "I believe that is checkmate, my friend."

Braddock looked at the board for a couple of seconds, then said, "Huh. You suckered me. I didn't see that coming."

"You are off your game. But don't worry. You're still recovering. You will be your old self again in no time."

Braddock wasn't sure about that. Two weeks had passed since that hellacious couple of days in El Paso and Juarez. He had lost weight, making him more whip-like lean than ever, and he hadn't regained his full strength yet. Luckily, things had been peaceful in Esperanza.

He wondered how things were in Santa Rosalia, as the people there tried to recover from the damage wreaked on their lives by Palmer, Hernandez, and Larrizo. At least he had seen all the women safely home as he had promised, including Carmen, before heading back to Esperanza and practically collapsing on the padre's doorstep.

"Another game?" the priest asked.

Braddock shook his head and said, "Not now. I reckon I've had all the beating I can take for one day."

The padre laughed and started to put away the board and the pieces. Braddock stood up and went to the door of his little house, which stood open to let in the breeze.

He frowned as he looked across the arid landscape and saw a rooster tail of dust rising from it. As he watched, the dust moved closer to the village.

"Somebody coming," he said.

"A harmless traveler, no doubt," the padre said, but a worried frown creased his forehead despite the words.

"We don't get many of those around here." Braddock took a Winchester down from a couple of pegs set into the adobe wall. He wasn't wearing a Colt, but he figured the rifle would do in case of trouble.

The padre sighed and said, "If it is someone else who wants you to go off tilting at windmills again, I wish you would tell them no, G.W. You are in no shape to be risking your life again so soon." He stood. "Let me go out and meet them, see what they want."

"No. You go on back home while you can, Padre."

The priest still looked worried, but he tucked the chessboard and the bag with the pieces under his arm and hurried out. Braddock stood in the jacal's doorway, leaning against the jamb, and watched the rooster tail come closer.

The dark speck at the bottom of it resolved itself into a buggy being pulled by a couple of horses. At least it wasn't an army of gunmen come to kill him and wipe out the village, he thought.

In fact, there seemed to be only one person in the buggy, and as the vehicle rolled closer, Braddock thought he caught a glint of sunlight shining on fair hair.

A few minutes later, Elizabeth Jane Caldwell pulled the buggy team to a stop in front of the jacal and waved a gloved hand in front of her face to swipe some of the dust away.

"You already sent the money you owed me," Braddock said, "and I sent you that letter telling you everything that happened, like I promised. What are you doing here, Miss Caldwell? How'd you even find the place?"

"I'm a journalist," she told him. "I have ways of finding things out. And that's not a very friendly greeting, Mr. Braddock."

"Most of the time, I'm not a very friendly man."

She climbed down from the buggy, brushed her hands off against each other, and said, "Well, despite that, I began to feel guilty and decided to come and check on you. I'm the one who got you into that dreadful mess. In a way, it's my fault you were injured so badly."

Braddock shook his head. “Not really. I think the fellas who actually tried to kill me deserve more of the blame.”

She came closer and looked up at him. “How are you doing?”

“I’m all right. Some days are better than others. Still got a ways to go, I reckon—”

“Amigo, is there a problem?”

The question made Braddock look over to where the padre stood with several of the men of the village beside him. A couple of them carried machetes, and one had an old blunderbuss in his hands.

Elizabeth glanced nervously at them. “You have friends here,” she said.

“They look out for me,” Braddock said. He chuckled and told the priest, “It’s fine, Padre. Señorita Caldwell didn’t come here to kill me.” He looked at her again. “Although I’m still not sure why you *are* here.”

“I’ve come to take care of you while you recuperate. I told you, I’m a good journalist, but in a pinch I’m a damned fine nurse, too.”

“You know,” Braddock said as he smiled and moved aside to let her come in, “I’ll bet you are.”

OUTLAW RANGER:

THE LAST WAR CHIEF

Chapter 1

He remembers the screams of women, children, and horses. Especially the horses squealing in agony as they are shot down by the blue-clad soldiers who come thundering down the canyon on their own mounts, the rifles in their hands belching fire and smoke.

The Comanche are horsemen. The death of the horses means the death of the people.

That death takes longer to find those proud riders who are now a-foot. It steals over them slowly as they are rounded up and herded north and east like animals themselves, into what was known then as Indian Territory but is now called Oklahoma. Despair saps the life from them, making them a shadow of what they once were, until they might as well not be Comanche.

He was a young man then, when the cavalry brought death to the canyon of the hard wood where his people made their home. A young man, but already a leader of his people, a war chief who had ridden with Quanah at the place the white men called Adobe Walls. What times those had been, before the medicine turned bad—

"Hey. Wake up, you ol' sumbitch. You can't sleep there. Move your red ass."

He tried to lift his head from the plank sidewalk, but his strength failed him. He murmured something in his native tongue. More than half asleep, he wasn't sure himself what he was saying.

A booted foot thudded into his ribs and rocked him over onto his side. Pain flooded through him, but it was a dull, distant ache, as if his senses were too old and feeble for him to really feel it. He managed to lift a gnarled hand and tried to wave away his tormentor.

"Damn it, I done told you before about gettin' drunk and sleepin' on the sidewalk, Pete. You're gonna make me drag you down to the jailhouse and lock you up, ain't you?"

"Pahitti Puuku," the old man said. Greasy gray hair straggled in front of his watery eyes as he finally succeeded in lifting his head. He peered through that screen at the lanky figure of Deputy Hal Vickery.

The deputy leaned closer and asked, "What'd you say?"

"Pahitti Puuku."

"You know I don't understand that redskin lingo."

"It means...Three Horses. It is...my name."

"Yeah, well, I'm gonna keep on callin' you Old Pete like ever'body else in Dinsmore. Now, can you get on your feet and stumble outta here? Because if I have to pick you up, you're goin' to a cell, I can promise you that."

Three Horses was a little more awake and alert now. His head pounded from the whiskey, and his side ached from the deputy's kick. But he was a war chief. He had suffered much worse in battle. He put his hands on the planks and pushed.

Deputy Vickery watched impatiently as Three Horses struggled to stand up. After what seemed like a long time and probably was, the old man was on his feet. He was considerably shorter than the lawman. The width of his shoulders testified to the fact that once he had been a powerful man, but the years had stolen much of his strength and caused his flesh to waste away.

At first glance it seemed that not a single inch of his face was free of wrinkles. He wore denim trousers and a faded blue cotton shirt, and the worst indignity of all, white man's shoes on his feet. Even after all this time, he longed for the supple hide of a good pair of moccasins.

"I am...up," he said.

"Good. Stay that way until you can stumble back to that shack o' yours. Can't have you clutterin' up the boardwalk that way. Hell, it's the Twentieth Century now, although I reckon a dumb redskin like you wouldn't know anything about that. Dinsmore's a modern town now."

It was true. The settlement, originally nothing more than a wide place in the trail, now boasted a two-story stone jail and an even bigger courthouse, along with a couple of blocks of businesses along the north side of the street, one of them the drugstore in front of which Three Horses had laid down and gone to sleep. Up at the end of the block was an impressive red-brick building that housed the bank that had been organized a couple of years earlier. Perched at the edge of the South Plains, with the rugged escarpment of the Caprock dropping away just east of town, Dinsmore was poised to grow into the biggest town between Fort Worth and Lubbock.

It wasn't the sort of place where a pathetic old drunken Indian was welcome anymore...not that the man everybody called Old Pete had been that welcome to start with. Nobody had ever summoned up the energy to run him off permanently, though.

Three Horses took a stumbling step. Deputy Vickery reached out and took hold of his shoulders to turn him around.

"Your shack's that way," the deputy said. "Now skedaddle. I got things to do."

With the work shoes shuffling along the planks, Three Horses started along the sidewalk.

He saw the men riding in from the direction of the Caprock but didn't really pay attention to them until they brought their horses to a stop in the street close to where Three Horses was making his laborious way.

"Look at that, Clete," one of the men said. "That's an old Indian, ain't it?"

"Really old," replied the rider whose name, evidently, was Clete. "Must be a hundred years old."

That showed how much the foolish white man knew. This was Three Horses' fifty-fourth summer. Or his fifty-third. He wasn't sure anymore. White man counted time in odd ways.

"I'm gonna talk to him," the first man said, grinning.

"Jawing with some old redskin isn't why we're here, Riggs."

"Won't take but a minute." Riggs swung a leg over his saddle and dropped lithely to the ground. He stepped up onto the sidewalk and went on, "Hey, chief, how you doin'?"

Three Horses frowned in surprise. How did this white man know he was a chief? There was a time when anyone could have told from the beadwork on his buckskins and the feathers in his headdress that he was a leader of his people, but the clothes he wore now were very different.

Still, this man recognized him for what he was, and that made Three Horses stand up a little straighter. He blinked several times, then said in the white man's tongue, "It is a good day. I am Pahitti Puuku, last war chief of the Comanche."

The man laughed, then said to his companions, "You hear that? He ain't just a dirty old redskin. We got ourselves an actual war chief here!"

"Come on, Riggs," Clete said. "Get back on your horse."

"I will, I will. I ain't never seen a real Comanche war chief, though." Riggs leaned closer and grinned at Three Horses. "Do a war dance."

"I am not at war," Three Horses said. "And it is the young warriors who dance."

"Well, you ain't young, that's for sure, but I reckon we can do something about the other part." Without warning, Riggs slapped Three Horses across the face. "How about now? Feel like lettin' out a war whoop and doin' a dance?"

Three Horses tried to step around the white man. He muttered, "Leave me alone."

Riggs put a hand on his chest and gave him a shove that made him stagger back a couple of steps. Then the white man slapped Three Horses again.

"You're gonna do a war dance, old man, whether you like it or not."

The second slap had been hard enough to make Three Horses' head swim dizzily. He had to catch hold of one of the posts holding up the wooden awning over the boardwalk to keep himself from falling. Anger tried to well up inside him, but he couldn't bring it to the surface. That would have taken too much effort, and he was too tired.

"Damn it," Clete said. He swung down from the saddle, handed the reins to one of the other men, and stepped up onto the planks. Three Horses thought Clete might make Riggs leave him alone, but instead the man swung a fist hard into his stomach. The blow made Three Horses double over, and that was too much for him to overcome. He toppled forward onto the planks and lay curled up around the pain in his middle.

"Aw, hell!" Riggs said. "What'd you go and do that for?"

"I figured it was the fastest way to get your mind off this ancient savage," Clete said. "Now come on, unless you'd rather ride by yourself from now on."

"Shoot, I never said that. I'm comin'."

Riggs paused just long enough to kick Three Horses, on the other side from where Deputy Vickery had kicked him before. At least the pain was balanced now.

Three Horses didn't know how long he lay there, unable to get up, before the shooting started.

Chapter 2

Part of Hal Vickery's job as deputy sheriff of Dinsmore County was to keep track of the comings and goings of strangers in the settlement. The town wasn't big enough yet to have its own marshal, although some of the businessmen had started talking about it, especially Cyrus McLemore, the president of the bank. The county sheriff was responsible for keeping the peace in town, and Sheriff Thane Warner had given that job to Vickery. Warner had two other deputies who helped him take care of trouble elsewhere in the county.

So Vickery was just doing his duty when he took note of the strangers who rode into Dinsmore from the east. He did a quick head count: eight of them. You usually didn't see that many men riding together on horseback unless they all worked for the same ranch and had come into town to blow off steam on payday.

Today wasn't payday. That was still three days off. It wasn't even a Saturday, which sometimes brought more folks into town than usual. It was Tuesday morning, still fairly early.

Vickery frowned as he wondered if he ought to go meet the men and inquire as to the business that had brought them to town. But then one of them said something and the whole bunch stopped. From where he stood leaning against an awning post in the middle of the next block, the deputy couldn't make out the words.

Vickery continued watching as the man who had spoken dismounted and stepped up onto the sidewalk to talk to Old Pete. The Indian's shack was on the eastern edge of town—just out of town, really, almost on the edge of the Caprock—and he'd finally been headed in the right direction. Vickery felt a little bad about losing his temper and kicking Pete. It was just that he had told the old-timer over and over again about getting drunk and falling asleep in public. Folks didn't like that.

Most people in Dinsmore barely tolerated Pete, anyway. He was willing to do any sort of odd job, no matter how unpleasant, and he didn't charge much, so he came in handy if you needed a privy mucked out or some animal carcass removed. Because of that, people put up with his boasting.

When he was drunk, he liked to go on about how he was the last war chief of the Comanche tribe and how he'd fought with ol' Quanah and then snuck off from the reservation up in what used to be Indian Territory. He claimed that all the land hereabouts was the rightful hunting ground of his people and said that they would take it back, one of these days when the buffalo herds returned.

Vickery wasn't going to hold his breath waiting for that to happen.

The stranger who had gotten off his horse was talking to Old Pete. Suddenly, the man slapped him. That was a mean thing to do, and it made Vickery's frown deepen as he straightened from his casual stance leaning on the post. Pete might be a smelly, troublesome old fool, but he was *Dinsmore's* smelly, troublesome old fool. No stranger could ride into town and start pushing him around.

Then Vickery hesitated. He had hauled off and kicked Pete not that long ago, after all. He knew how annoying the old Indian could be. Maybe, if the fella would leave him alone, it would be better to just let things go.

Then the man slapped Pete again.

Vickery wasn't going to stand for that. He started along the boardwalk. But he didn't get in too big a hurry about it. Even though it was only mid-morning, the day was already hot, and a fella didn't want to rush around too much in the West Texas heat. It wasn't good for the blood.

One of the other men dismounted. Vickery hoped he would take his companion in hand. The whole bunch might move on.

Then the second man punched Pete in the belly, an even more despicable blow than the others. Pete fell down, and the first man kicked him. Vickery really felt bad now about what he'd done, as he watched somebody else do the same thing. That was pretty sorry behavior.

"Hey!" he called as he stepped off the end of the boardwalk in this block and started across the open space between the buildings. All eight of the strangers turned toward him, and he heard the man who had kicked Pete say, "Oh, hell, Riggs, now look what you've done. A lawman."

Vickery was about to say that damn right he was a lawman and he wasn't going to stand for any of Dinsmore's citizens being treated that way, but then the second man lifted his arm and there was a gun in his hand, a gun the deputy hadn't even seen him draw. Vickery stopped short as his eyes widened and he reached for the revolver on his hip.

He had just closed his hand around the gun butt when he heard the blast of a shot at the same time as what felt like a sledgehammer struck him in the chest. He went over backward, and the act of falling helped him pull his gun from its holster. His arm sort of flew upward of its own accord, but he was conscious of pulling the trigger. He heard shots booming like thunderclaps in a spring storm.

That was the last thing he knew.

Chapter 3

The shots were so loud they seemed to shake the planks Three Horses was lying on, and somehow that jolted the pain out of him. The racket also blew away the last lingering effects of the whiskey he had stolen early that morning while he was sweeping out the Three Deuces, Dinsmore's only saloon. The place didn't have a regular swamper, but Three Horses swept and mopped there two or three times a week, and Miles Bowen, the owner, usually turned a blind eye when he snagged a bottle that still had a little booze in it and tucked it inside his shirt.

For one thing, when he let Three Horses get away with that, Bowen usually didn't bother paying him. The rotgut didn't cost much since Bowen brewed it himself in an old bathtub, throwing in some black powder, strychnine, and rattlesnake heads for flavor.

Sober now, or as close to it as he got these days, Three Horses lifted his head, pushed himself up on his elbows, and looked along Dinsmore's single street. He saw somebody lying in the open space between the two blocks of businesses, and he needed a second or two before he recognized the sprawled figure in the bloody shirt as Deputy Hal Vickery.

Despite everything that had happened earlier, Three Horses felt a pang of regret at the sight. Vickery sometimes got mad and treated him badly, but the deputy has helped him at times, too, taking pity on him and getting him back to his shack when he was too drunk to make it there under his own power.

The eight strangers—Clete, Riggs, and the other six men—were doing most of the shooting. Four of them, including Clete and Riggs, were standing in front of the bank pouring lead through the windows and the open front door.

The other four were still on their horses as they fired toward the jail. Their mounts were a little skittish, so they had to divide their efforts between controlling the animals and shooting at the stone building.

Little puffs of gunsmoke came from one of the jail's front windows. Three Horses didn't know where the sheriff and the other two deputies were, but it seemed likely at least one man was inside, putting up a fight.

Everyone else who had been on the street when the trouble started—and there hadn't been that many—had vanished, immediately hunting cover as the bullets began to fly.

Bill Denning, who owned the drugstore, proved to be the exception to that. He emerged from the front door of his business and stomped along the sidewalk past Three Horses carrying an old Henry rifle. He yelled, "Damn thieves!" and brought the repeater to his shoulder. It cracked once, but none of the strangers fell.

One of them on horseback yanked his mount around toward the walk, however, and the revolver in his hand let out two heavy booms. Denning flew backward to land next to Three Horses, who was lying on his belly. The front of the storekeeper's apron Denning wore over his clothes was bloody, and a good chunk of his head was blown away. His eyes were wide open as he stared sightlessly up at the awning.

If anybody else in town was thinking about fighting back against the outlaws, the sight of Denning being killed in such a grisly fashion put a stop to that.

Except for Three Horses, who looked over at the Henry the drugstore owner had dropped and felt an unexpected longing.

Years ago, Three Horses had had a rifle like that. He had taken it from a dead settler on a ranch he and some other warriors had raided up on the Double Mountain fork of the Brazos. The weapon had seemed like magic at the time, a gun that could shoot all day without having to be reloaded.

Of course there was no magic to it—the white men had no real magic—and the Comanches had figured that out and soon lost their fear of the repeaters. In fact, many warriors had become quite proficient in their use.

Three Horses had been good with a rifle. But he recalled how heavy a Henry was, and how his hands shook and the muscles in his arms trembled when he tried to lift too much these days, and he decided it wouldn't be a good idea.

Just to be sure none of the outlaws would think he had anything in mind, he let his head droop back to the planks and lay there like he was senseless.

He kept his eyes slitted open, though, and watched as Clete and Riggs and the other two men on foot rushed into the bank. They must have killed everyone inside, thought Three Horses.

Then two more shots sounded, first one and then a second blast a couple of heartbeats later, and Three Horses thought, no, *now* they have killed everyone.

The shooting from the jail stopped as well. An echoing silence hung over the settlement. A minute went by. Two. Three.

Then Clete and Riggs and the other two ran out of the bank. Clete had a gun in each hand, but the others each carried a pair of canvas sacks. Three Horses knew the bags were full of money.

He frowned as he forced his brain to work. Was payday coming up soon? It was, he decided. The bank usually had plenty of cash on hand for that, since there were a number of large ranches in the area with big crews that collected wages once a month.

Working quickly, without any wasted effort, the outlaws tied the money bags to their saddles and swung up. Clete, who seemed to be the leader, was the last one in the saddle. He pouched his left-hand iron and grabbed the reins, swinging his horse around and jabbing his boot heels in its flanks.

The entire gang galloped toward Three Horses.

He was convinced they were going to shoot him as they raced past. Terror gnawed at his guts.

Then he felt something different and realized it was shame burning inside him because he was afraid. There had been a time when he felt no fear, even when he was facing many enemies. If he was truly a warrior, truly a man, he told himself, he would take that rifle and stand up and fight...

The outlaws veered into the open space between the blocks, making the turn with the skill of expert horsemen, and charged out of town as if they intended to head north along the Caprock.

As they did, the steel-shod hooves of their mounts chopped and pounded the body of Deputy Hal Vickery until it looked like a heap of bloody rags instead of something human.

Then they were gone, the swift rataplan of hoofbeats fading into the distance.

Three Horses heard someone weeping. He had to think about it for a while before he realized the wretched sounds came from him. He didn't know if he was crying for Deputy Vickery and everyone else the strangers had killed in Dinsmore on this hot Tuesday morning, or for himself because they had humiliated him and he had done nothing about it except lie there and wallow in his own fear.

It was a bad day for the once-proud Comanche people when their last war chief acted that way, he thought. The latest bad day in a very long line of them.

Chapter 4

G.W. Braddock was a long way from the border. Too far for safety, really. Despite the badge pinned to his faded blue bib-front shirt, he was a wanted man on this side of the Rio Grande.

An outlaw, not a Texas Ranger anymore.

But that didn't mean he could stop enforcing the law. It was the job he had been raised to do, after all, and no amount of political shenanigans designed to cripple the Ranger force could change that.

These days, he had a home of sorts in the Mexican village of Esperanza, just across the border. The priest at the mission there had nursed Braddock back to health from the wounds he had received defending the village from marauders. The little brown-robed padre was the closest thing Braddock had to a friend in this world, he supposed.

From time to time, when word reached the village of trouble in Texas, Braddock pinned on the star-in-a-circle badge carved from a Mexican *cinco peso* coin, and rode back across the river to the land of his birth, the land he had been raised to serve. The most recent occasion had been several weeks earlier. One of the farmers from the village had ventured downriver to Del Rio to sell some crops on the Texas side, and he had returned to Esperanza with the tale of how a gang of vicious outlaws had robbed the bank there while the farmer was in town.

The leader of the gang, it was said, was a man named Clete Fenner.

Braddock knew the name, even though he had never crossed trails with the desperado. He remembered seeing it in the Doomsday Book, the Ranger "bible" that listed all the known lawbreakers in the state.

It was time that name was crossed out of the book, Braddock

had decided. When he heard how wantonly Fenner and his men had shot up Del Rio, that made up his mind for him. That group of mad dogs had to be stopped.

Braddock had picked up the trail without much trouble, but closing in on Fenner's gang was a different story. Somehow, the outlaws managed to stay one or two jumps ahead of him, even when they stopped long enough to hit a bank or rob a stagecoach or steal some fresh horses from a ranch.

They left a trail of bodies behind them as well, and each brutal, senseless death added to Braddock's resolve. He would bring the killers to justice no matter how far he had to follow them.

That was how he wound up several hundred miles north of the border, riding northwest as he approached the Caprock, the line of rugged bluffs that ran in irregular fashion through this region, dividing Central Texas from the windswept plains that stretched all the way from here to New Mexico Territory. Fenner and his men had been spotted heading in this direction, following the wagon road.

Wherever they were bound for, they wouldn't have anything good in mind when they got there.

The trail dropped down into a little depression just this side of the escarpment, then started up. The rocky bluff was dotted with brush, but lots of bare ground showed through as well, and in the midday sun the red clay common to this area was vividly bright. Up on the plains, it would be a different story, Braddock knew. The soil there was sandier, more thickly covered with vegetation lying close to the ground. It was good grazing land, although it became more arid the farther west a man went.

The climb was steep in places as the trail twisted back and forth, but not too steep for a horse. Braddock reached the top and reined in as he saw a settlement lying less than half a mile away. A lot of people were moving around in the single street, he thought as a slight frown creased his forehead. More than seemed normal even though it was the middle of the day and folks might be out and about.

He heeled the dun forward.

Braddock had the broad shoulders and lean hips of a born

horseman. A lot of time spent in the saddle as he chased badmen around Texas had allowed the sun to bestow a brown, leathery look to his face. It had faded his hair and mustache to a sandy color. A scar on his forehead disappeared up under his darker brown hat. A saber belonging to a crazed *rurale capitan* had left the mark there.

Like the hat, his clothes were typical dust-covered range garb. He wore a Colt .45 in a holster on his right hip, and the well-worn wooden stock of a Winchester repeater stuck up from a sheath lashed to his saddle.

The only bright thing about him was the Ranger badge. It glittered in the sun. When people saw it, they recognized the authority it carried and tended not to notice the small, neat bullet hole in the center of it, a souvenir from another encounter with a killer. They assumed that Braddock was still an official lawman, not an outlaw, and it suited his purposes not to correct that assumption.

He had to be careful about other star-packers, though. Often they were more alert and suspicious than civilians.

But not the one Braddock found in this settlement. This one was running around like a chicken with its head cut off.

The man was a little below medium height and stocky. His round face had what looked like a permanent sunburn. That went with the blue eyes and the fair hair under a thumbed-back hat. He had a badge pinned to his shirt.

When he spotted Braddock, he stopped hurrying around among the various groups of townspeople in the street and on the plank sidewalk. A look of relief came over his face. He started walking toward Braddock and was almost running by the time he got there.

"You're a Ranger?" the man said. "A Texas Ranger?"

"That's right," Braddock said. In his heart he would always be a Ranger, no matter what the official records in Austin said. Now that he was closer, he could read the words *DEPUTY SHERIFF* etched on the tin star. "What happened here, Deputy?"

The man took off his hat and scrubbed a pudgy-fingered hand over his flushed face. He heaved a sigh, as if exhaustion were catching up to him.

"Bank robbers," he said. "A gang of outlaws hit the bank about an hour ago."

"Anybody hurt?" asked Braddock.

"They killed seven people, including Sheriff Warner and Deputy Vickery," the man replied. "My name's Andy Bell. I'm the only law left here in Dinsmore. At least, I was until you showed up, Ranger...?"

"Braddock," he introduced himself curtly. "Dinsmore is the name of this settlement?"

"Yeah."

"I've heard of it, I reckon. Never been here before, that I recall." Braddock nodded toward the stone courthouse. "It's the county seat, I see."

"Yeah. The biggest town in the county. And the only one with a bank." Deputy Bell made a face. "I reckon that's why those sons o' bitches came here."

"How many of them were there?"

"Eight or ten. I've gotten different answers from people. It's hard to keep count when something like that's going on. They shot Deputy Vickery first." Bell pointed to a blanket-shrouded figure lying in the street between the two blocks of businesses. A couple of booted feet stuck out from under the blanket. "Then some of them opened fire on the sheriff's office and jail while the others shot through the bank's front windows until everybody inside was either dead or wounded. They went in then and cleaned out the cash drawers and the vault and...and finished off the wounded."

"The vault was open?" Braddock asked.

Deputy Bell shrugged and said, "This is a little town. Nothing like this ever happened here. Nobody figured it ever would." Bell paused and swallowed hard. "They didn't have to kill everybody. They could have gone in, held up the place at gunpoint, and gotten the money if that was all they were after. It was like they...they *wanted* to slaughter innocent people."

"This gang...was the leader named Fenner? Clete Fenner?"

Bell's shoulders rose and fell in a shrug.

"Mister, I just couldn't tell you. I don't know if anybody heard any of them call the others by name. I've been askin' questions, but it all happened so fast, and like I told you, nobody ever expected anything like this..."

Braddock held up a hand to stop Bell before the deputy could force himself to go on. Bell might be fine for serving legal papers or guarding prisoners, but when faced with a real catastrophe, he didn't seem like much of a lawman.

But maybe he shouldn't judge people, Braddock told himself. After all, at least Bell had a legal right to wear his badge.

"You say the sheriff was killed?"

"Yes, sir. When he heard the commotion going on outside, he stepped through the door to find out what it was all about and caught a couple of slugs in the chest right away. He fell in the doorway and I was able to get hold of his shirt and drag him the rest of the way back inside without getting shot myself." Bell shook his head. "Wasn't anything I could do for him, though. He was already gone. All I could do was fort up at one of the windows and try to wing some of that bunch, but I don't know if I did or not. They made it pretty hot for me."

"Who else was killed?"

"Like I said, the folks in the bank. Mr. McLemore, the president, and Ben Horton, the teller, along with a couple of customers. And Mr. Denning, who owned the drugstore. He came out and took a shot at 'em, and they gunned him down, just shot him like a dog."

Braddock said, "I'll bet nobody put up a fight after that, did they?"

"No, sir, they did not. And I, for one, don't really blame 'em."

"Didn't say I blamed them. They just would have gotten themselves killed if they had, without doing anybody else any good. From the sound of it, that was the Fenner gang, all right. I've been on their trail for weeks. I could count up the number of people they've killed, I suppose, but it would make me a little sick."

"So you're going after them?" Deputy Bell asked. Braddock heard an almost pathetic eagerness in the man's voice. If a Texas Ranger took over the pursuit, that would relieve Bell of the responsibility for doing so.

"Like I said, I've been on their trail. This just makes me more determined than ever to catch up to them. You haven't put together a posse yet, have you?"

"No, I was just thinking about gettin' around to doing that..."

"Don't," Braddock said.

Bell frowned and said, "I beg your pardon?"

"I'll go after them alone. I don't need a posse."

What Braddock meant but didn't say was that he didn't need a posse slowing him down and cluttering things up. He could move faster alone, and he wouldn't have to worry about a bunch of inexperienced townies getting themselves killed when he finally caught up to Fenner's bunch.

"Are you sure? I mean, it was our town they hit, our bank they robbed. Our people they killed—"

"They've done the same thing across a wide swath of Texas. Don't worry, they'll get what's coming to them."

"But...but it'll be eight or ten to one..."

"Long odds never bothered me," Braddock said.

An outlaw Ranger couldn't expect to live forever.

Chapter 5

The long journey had depleted Braddock's supplies, so he figured it would be a good idea to replenish them here in Dinsmore before setting off after Clete Fenner and his gang. If his pursuit of the outlaws had taught him anything, it was that he couldn't predict how long it was going to take him to corral them.

Several of Dinsmore's citizens came up to him while he was in the general store and offered to come with him. Word had gotten around quickly that there was a Texas Ranger in town who planned to go after the bank robbers.

Braddock refused the offers of assistance as diplomatically as he could, but he knew he was a little curt to some of the men. He couldn't worry about that. Time was a-wasting. With every minute that passed, the bloodthirsty gang would be getting farther away.

So he was in no mood to be delayed when he stepped out onto the sidewalk in front of the store with a canvas sack of supplies in his hand and an old-timer waiting there lifted a trembling hand to stop him.

"Ranger," the man said. "I must talk to you."

With the old man blocking his path, Braddock had no choice but to stop. He saw that the man was an Indian and realized he might not be as quite as old as Braddock had thought at first. Or he might be older. With all those wrinkles in the weathered skin, it was hard to tell. The fellow might have been anywhere from fifty to eighty.

"I'm in a hurry—" Braddock began.

"You are going after the man called Clete?"

That question made Braddock frown for a second. He said, "How do you know one of them was named Clete?"

Of course, he had mentioned the name to Deputy Bell, he recalled, and he didn't know who Bell might have told. The old

Indian could have heard it that way.

"I heard one of them say it," the old-timer replied. "And Clete called that one Riggs."

Braddock's interest quickened. This leathery old cuss might know something useful after all.

"You heard them talking to each other?"

"They spoke...to me." The old man rested his right hand against his narrow chest with the fingers splayed out.

"What did they say?"

"The one called Riggs, he asked me to do a war dance."

"Why would he do that?" asked Braddock.

"Because I am Three Horses, last war chief of the Comanche."

Braddock managed not to snort in disbelief. The old man was short and wiry. Scrawny might have been a better description. He wore a ragged work shirt and trousers and scuffed shoes that probably had holes in the soles. Shaggy gray hair hung over his eyes and ears. He looked about as far from being a war chief as anybody could get.

"Did you hear them say anything about where they were headed from here?"

Three Horses, if that was really his name, shook his head.

"No. Riggs slapped me, to try to get me to dance, and then the one called Clete, he hit me, too, and knocked me down so Riggs would leave me alone. Clete was angry and told him they had to get on with their business."

Yeah, the business of robbing the bank and murdering half a dozen innocent people, thought Braddock.

"I saw what they did," Three Horses went on. "After Clete knocked me down, I was lying on the sidewalk, there, in front of the drugstore where Mr. Denning was killed. I did not get up."

Braddock grunted and said, "Good thing you didn't. They probably would've shot you, too."

"I looked at the rifle Mr. Denning had. I thought about fighting them. I could have done it." Three Horses looked down at the sidewalk. "But I did nothing."

"Well, that's all right, old-timer. Fighting outlaws isn't your job. It's mine."

Braddock moved to step around him, but once again the old Indian lifted a hand to stop him.

"Among my people, I was always one of the best trackers. On the hunt, I could follow prey across many miles." Three Horses made a sweeping gesture with his hand, like a Wild West Show Indian putting on a show. "No enemy ever escaped me once I had found his trail. I will come with you, Ranger, and help you track down these evil men."

The offer took Braddock by surprise. The Indian looked like he was barely strong enough to walk down the street, let alone trail a gang of vicious killers across the plains.

"I appreciate that," Braddock said, "but you don't need to—"

Three Horses moved closer and said, "They struck me. They knocked me down and then they kicked me, like I was a mongrel dog that had slunk in their way. They did this to me, Three Horses, last war chief of the Comanche." He drew himself up straighter and glared. "They must be punished."

"Yeah, well, I plan to see to it," Braddock told him. "You can count on that. But I don't need any help."

"There are eight of them," Three Horses said with conviction.

"You're sure of that?"

"I counted them. Four attacked the bank, the other four attacked the sheriff's office."

That jibed well enough with what Deputy Bell had told him, Braddock thought. He was willing to accept what Three Horses said about how many outlaws there had been, although it didn't really change things one way or the other.

However many there were, Braddock still had to bring them to justice or die trying.

"Thanks anyway, Three Horses, but I ride alone."

"Because of that?"

The old man pointed at the badge on Braddock's shirt. Braddock frowned and said, "What do you mean?"

"The hole in that badge...it means you are apart from all the other Rangers. Is this not true?"

Braddock started to brush past him, muttering, "I've got to get riding—"

"You are the only one of your kind," Three Horses persisted, "just as I am the last war chief of my people. That is why you ride alone. Perhaps two who ride alone...should ride together."

"Forget it," Braddock said. He headed for the dun. "Go back to whatever it is you do around here."

Behind him, Three Horses was silent.

Deputy Bell came up while Braddock was tying the supplies behind his saddle. The lawman said, "Are you sure you don't want me to come with you, Ranger?"

"No, you don't need to leave the town without any law. After a tragedy like this, folks need to see that there's still somebody in charge."

"I never thought that'd be me," Bell said. He took a bandanna from his pocket and wiped sweat off his face. "I'm the youngest of the three deputies. Hal Vickery, he was in charge of keepin' order here in town, and he's dead. Gene Dixon, he's chief deputy. Sheriff Warner sent him down to the southern part of the county to look for some cattle thieves. Probably won't be back for a few days. That just leaves me."

"You'll be fine," Braddock told him, although in truth he hoped that nothing else bad happened in Dinsmore until that older deputy got back. Bell might find himself over his head pretty easily.

The deputy didn't look convinced by Braddock's reassurances, but he said, "I saw Old Pete talking to you. Sorry if he bothered you."

"The old Indian? He said his name was Three Horses."

"Yeah, but most of the time he spouts the Comanche version of it, and nobody can pronounce that so folks started calling him Old Pete. Maybe that other name means Three Horses, but you couldn't prove it by me. I don't speak Comanch'."

Braddock said, "Was he really a war chief?"

"Who the hell knows? You've seen him. He's just a drunken old sot and a part-time handyman. Showed up here about five years ago and he's been hanging around ever since, making a pest of himself. What did he want, anyway?"

"He wanted to come with me. Wanted to help me track Fenner and his gang."

Bell's pale eyebrows went up as he said, "You're not taking him along, are you?"

"Not hardly," Braddock said.

Chapter 6

The Caprock rose anywhere from five hundred to two thousand feet above the rolling, scrub-covered terrain to the east. The outlaws' trail ran close enough to the rim that Braddock had a spectacular view in that direction. Some people might say the landscape was ugly, but Braddock found a stark beauty in it. He was a Texan, born, bred, and forever, and just about everywhere in the Lone Star State had something to recommend it, as far as he was concerned.

There wasn't much in the direction he was headed except some isolated ranches. Maybe Fenner and his gang were going to ground at long last, after their bloody trek from the border country. With all the robberies they had carried out, they had to have a pretty good stash of loot by now. They might hole up somewhere, wait for any pursuit to die down, and then venture out to enjoy their ill-gotten gains somewhere like Denver or San Francisco.

They might even scatter to the four winds, which would make it extremely difficult to track down all of them. Braddock wanted to catch up to the gang before that could happen. He pushed the dun as fast as he dared. The horse had covered a lot of ground in the past few weeks, however, and Braddock couldn't risk asking too much of him.

Red sandstone boulders littered the edge of the Caprock in places, and fissures cut into the escarpment's face. It was rugged country that could hide a lot of dangers, and Braddock was well aware of that and kept his eyes open.

Because he was alert, he saw afternoon sunlight reflect off something metal among a clump of large rock slabs. Letting his instincts take over instead of thinking about it, he leaned forward in the saddle and jabbed his boot heels in the dun's flanks. The horse leaped forward as a rifle cracked. Braddock heard a bullet whine just behind him as it ripped through the space where he had been a split-second earlier.

More shots crashed as Braddock galloped toward the nearest cover, some low rocks less than half as big as the boulders where the would-be killers were concealed. They had chosen a good spot for their ambush. The ground was bare and open except for some small mesquite trees that wouldn't really provide much concealment or stop bullets. The rocks were Braddock's only chance. He couldn't hope to outrun rifles.

Bullets kicked up dust around the dun's flashing hooves. Since they had missed their first couple of shots at him, they were trying to shoot the horse out from under him, Braddock knew. If they were able to do that, then they could pick him off at their leisure.

The dun was moving so fast it made a difficult target, though. The horse jumped a little as a slug burned across its rump, but that was the closest any of the bullets came. As they neared the rocks, Braddock pulled his Winchester from the saddle boot, kicked his feet free of the stirrups, and dived off the horse's back.

He lost his hat as he flew through the air. He landed running, lost his balance, went down, and rolled. A bullet whistled past his ear as he came up and lunged forward to stretch out on his belly among the rocks.

He hoped there weren't any rattlesnakes sunning themselves in there. Even if there were, they might be better company than a bunch of hot lead.

Braddock didn't hear any of the telltale buzzing that would have let him know he had scaly companions in this precarious sanctuary. Of course, the blood was pounding pretty loudly in his head by now, drowning out just about everything else. But as his pulse slowed, he heard the shots from the boulders about fifty yards away, the thud as bullets struck the rocks that protected him, and the occasional whine as a slug ricocheted off.

As long as he kept his head down, he was safe. Enough rocks were scattered around him to keep the bushwhackers from having a clear shot at him.

They must have realized they were wasting lead, because their rifles fell silent. Braddock lay there breathing hard as tense seconds crawled past.

They were trying to bait him into making a move, he thought. From the sounds of the shots, two men were hidden in the boulders, and he'd be willing to bet that both of them had their rifles aimed at the spot where he had disappeared. Their fingers would be tight on the triggers. If he raised his head, even for a second, they would fire, and it was even money whether or not they would blow his brains out.

So it was a waiting game. Braddock was pinned down, sure, but a glance at the sky told him there were only about five hours of daylight left. He would get mighty hot and thirsty in that time, baking here under the sun, but it wouldn't kill him. And when night fell, he would be able to move again.

He twisted his head around to look for his horse. The dun had kept running for about a quarter of a mile before coming to a stop. He stood there now, grazing aimlessly on clumps of hardy grass. At least the bushwhackers weren't shooting at him anymore. No reason to kill a perfectly good horse when his rider was the real target and that rider was no longer in the saddle.

Two men, Braddock mused as the back of his neck began to get warm. Hidden in the boulders along the rim like that, it was obvious they had been waiting for someone to come along. Him in particular? Braddock doubted it. More likely Clete Fenner had left a couple members of the gang to discourage any posse from Dinsmore that had followed them.

Braddock was only one man, not a posse, but maybe they had spotted him through field glasses and seen the badge on his shirt. They would know he was a lawman. They might have even figured out it was a Ranger badge.

Might have been better not to wear the thing, but it was part of who he was. That was why he had refused to turn it in or give up enforcing the law, the job he was born for, no matter what some judge or politician said.

Damn, the sun was hot, even though it wasn't directly overhead. Braddock wondered how much time had gone by. Seemed like an hour, but he knew that probably only a few minutes had passed.

If the two bushwhackers really wanted him dead, they would have to make a move before dark. They couldn't afford to just squat there in the boulders and wait. More than likely, one of them would try to flank him, move around so that he had a clear shot. Braddock listened intently for any sound that might warn him that was happening.

Suddenly, shots boomed out again, the echoes rolling across the Caprock and the valleys below. A distraction, thought Braddock. One of the killers was on the move.

He twisted, using his elbows and toes to wiggle himself over to a narrow gap between the rocks. He thrust the Winchester's barrel through the opening and waited. He knew it was fifty-fifty that the outlaw would go that direction, and even if he did, Braddock would have only a split-second to fire.

A flash of movement in the distance. Braddock had already taken the slight bit of slack out of the trigger. He squeezed it the rest of the way. The Winchester cracked wickedly as it bucked against his shoulder.

The shots from the boulders stopped. Braddock heard a man yelling in pain. A faint smile tugged at his lips under the mustache. Instinct—and one hell of a lot of luck, to be honest—must have guided his shot. He edged forward, trying to see if he could spot the man he had wounded, but his field of vision was too small, the angle too restricted.

A few moments later, both rifles opened up on his position again. The man he had winged must not have been hurt too badly. He had retreated into the boulders and joined his companion in an angry fusillade at the rocks where Braddock had taken cover. They were just venting their spleen. They still couldn't get a good shot at him.

Then he heard a boom and a startled shout. Braddock knew from the sound of the earlier reports that the bushwhackers were using Winchesters or Henrys. That shot hadn't come from a repeater. It had sounded more like a heavy caliber buffalo gun.

Somebody else was getting in on this fight.

The question was, on which side?

Chapter 7

From the door of his tar-paper shack, Three Horses watched the Ranger ride out of Dinsmore, heading north along the edge of the Caprock on the trail of the outlaws.

The Ranger had made a mistake. He should have accepted Three Horses' help. Three Horses was a tracker and a warrior. He would have given his life to help bring those men to justice.

Maybe he still could.

He turned and went to the bunk where he slept on a bare corn-shuck mattress. Bending over, he reached under the bunk and pulled out a rifle. It was very old. Rust pitted its barrel, and at some time in the past its stock had been cracked and then mended by having wire wrapped tightly around it. The breech and the bore were clean, though. Three Horses used a rag and a stick every day to wipe away the red dust that got into everything.

Many years earlier, the rifle had belonged to a buffalo hunter, a huge, bearded, shaggy man who resembled the beasts he stalked and slew. During a battle with a group of hunters who had taken cover in a buffalo wallow, Three Horses had counted coup on the man, then turned his pony to race back in and put an arrow through his throat. He had taken the rifle, which he had thought of then as a shoots-far-gun, as his by right, since he had killed its owner, just like the Henry he had taken from a dead rancher several years later.

By now he knew it was a .50 caliber Sharps. He had shot it a few times and never liked it, but he had wrapped it in a blanket and hidden it among the few possessions he'd been allowed to take along when his people were herded northeast to the reservation in Indian Territory. He could not have said why he hung on to it, other than the fact that he sensed there was powerful medicine in it, and one day that medicine would be revealed to him.

All he was certain of was that he could not leave it behind when he fled the reservation. He reached under the bunk again and pulled out the other thing he had brought with him, a white man's carpetbag filled with even more precious possessions.

He felt stronger now. The whiskey had sweated out through his skin. When he held his hands in front of his face, they trembled, but only a little.

Could he do this? Three Horses had to admit he didn't know. But he had to try.

Carrying the Sharps in his left hand and the carpetbag in his right, he walked back into town to the livery stable owned by Asa Edmonds. From time to time, Three Horses cleaned the stalls for Mr. Edmonds. He found the man sitting on a barrel just outside the barn's open double doors.

"Howdy, Pete," Edmonds said. "Hell of a thing, wasn't it? The way those outlaws came in and killed so many folks, I mean."

"Yes," Three Horses agreed. "A hell of a thing."

His people, as a rule, didn't curse, but you had to talk to white men in a language they understood.

Edmonds frowned at the carpetbag and the rifle. He asked, "You goin' somewhere? Takin' a trip?"

"Yes, I must leave Dinsmore for a time."

"Goin' back to the reservation?" The liveryman grinned. "You ain't goin' on the warpath, are you?"

"There is something I have to do."

"Well, don't let me stop you. You just go right ahead." Edmonds chuckled, as if the idea of an Indian having anything important to do amused him.

"I would like to borrow the mule, the one called Abner."

A frown replaced Edmonds' grin as he said, "Wait a minute. You want to borrow my mule? You mean rent it, don't you? I ain't in the business of lettin' folks *borrow* my animals."

Three Horses shook his head and said, "You know I have no money. But I will give you something in return for the loan of the mule."

He set the carpetbag down, leaned the Sharps against the wall, and opened the bag to take out a tomahawk. Its handle was decorated with bits of brightly colored rock and feathers tied on with rawhide.

Edmonds' eyes opened wider as he said, "That looks real."

"It is real. It belonged to Satanta. He gave it to me himself, for saving his life during a battle with the bluecoats, before they took him later on and hung him."

That was a lie in more ways than one. Three Horses had made the tomahawk himself, just to pass the time during the dreary days on the reservation. He had never met the notorious warrior Satanta.

But Edmonds didn't know that, and he let out a low whistle.

"You're sayin' you'll gimme that if I let you borrow Abner?"

Three Horses nodded and said solemnly, "Yes."

"But I don't have to return it, even when you bring Abner back."

"That is right. It is yours."

Three Horses held out the tomahawk, and the liveryman took it.

"You got yourself a deal," Edmonds said.

"You will provide a saddle, too?"

Edmonds frowned and said, "Dang, there must be somethin' to that idea that you Injuns are related to the Jews, the way you like to haggle. Ah, hell, sure, I'll throw in a saddle. Just not one of the good ones. Get one of 'em that's set aside in the tack room. You know the ones I mean."

Three Horses nodded and walked into the welcome shade of the barn. He went to the stall where Edmonds kept the mule Abner and led the animal out. Mules were supposed to be balky, but Abner and Three Horses had always gotten along well and Abner cooperated now. Three Horses got a ratty blanket and a saddle that needed mending from the tack room and soon had Abner ready to ride.

Edmonds was still sitting on the barrel, turning the tomahawk over in his hands. He looked up at Three Horses and said, "I've figured it out. You're gonna go hunt buffalo."

"When I hunted buffalo, I used a bow and arrow, not a gun."

"What's the rifle for, then?"

"To hunt men," Three Horses said.

He rode off and left the liveryman staring after him.

Chapter 8

It was amazing how much a man could change in less than a day's time. A matter of hours, really. When he had climbed out of his bunk this morning, Three Horses hadn't expected anything other than one more day of struggling to get by as he battled the demons inside him. One more day of cadging drinks, one more day of doing menial labor if he could find anyone willing to hire him, one more day of being humiliated and laughed at by people who didn't believe him when he told them what he had been in the past.

He had been humiliated and laughed at, all right, but he had also been beaten and kicked like a dog. He had stared into the face of death only inches from his, when the outlaw killed Denning. He had seen blood spilled and heard the cries of the grieving. He had felt the worm of fear inside him, eating away at his soul.

In the past, when anything this upsetting had happened, Three Horses had sought solace in a bottle. Solace and forgetfulness. There was nothing like whiskey to numb the pain of a man's pride as it slowly withered away.

So why was today different, he wondered as he rode along the rim of the Caprock? Perhaps some men reached the end of their rope and died, as he had expected to, while others grasped that rope and used it to pull themselves up.

Which would he be?

His eyes were not as sharp as they once had been, he discovered as he followed the trail left by the outlaws. At first he had no trouble, but as he continued north he found that from time to time he had to rein Abner to a halt, swing down from the saddle, and bend over with his hands on his knees to study the ground more closely. He didn't lose the trail, but the days when it would have been as plain as could be for him to see were long gone.

He had been riding for several hours. It had been quite a while since he had spent that much time on horseback, and his old bones were really starting to feel it. Maybe he should have ridden with just a blanket, as he had in his youth, he thought, but he had grown accustomed to using a saddle like a white man. He should have known better.

He was thirsty, too. A canteen full of water hung from the saddle horn, but Three Horses knew that wasn't what he wanted. When he lifted his hand to wipe the back of it across his mouth, he noticed that it was shaking a little more than it had been back in town, when he had decided to follow the Ranger and the outlaws. Maybe he ought to turn back, he thought. It wasn't too late.

That was when he heard the sharp cracks of rifle fire in the distance ahead of him.

Three Horses brought Abner to a stop and frowned. He could tell that at least two guns were going off, but Braddock hadn't caught up to the whole gang or else the sounds of battle would have been much greater. Still, Three Horses had no doubt that the Ranger was involved in the violent altercation going on somewhere up ahead.

He leaned forward and squinted. Perhaps a quarter of a mile away, he saw some large slabs of rock along the rim. That would be a good place for an ambush, he thought, remembering the days when he had lain in wait in just such a situation, ready to kill any white men unlucky enough to ride by.

Some of the outlaws could have ambushed Ranger Braddock, Three Horses decided. He had no idea where Braddock had taken cover, but the lawman had to be alive or else the shooting would have stopped.

He turned the mule toward the rim. It was time for stealth—and no one was stealthier than a Comanche war chief.

He found a cut that led down into the valley at a fairly gentle angle and rode Abner along it for a hundred yards. Then he stopped and tied the mule's reins to a bush. Taking the Sharps with him, Three Horses started walking along the sloping face of the escarpment, detouring to avoid areas that were too rocky or steep.

He wasn't exactly nimble-footed anymore and almost slipped and fell several times. But he made fairly good progress as the guns continued to blast above him. When he judged that he was almost even with them, he turned and started to climb back toward the rim.

He reached it not far from the rocks he had seen earlier. Staying low, he lifted his head just enough to see two men hidden behind the slabs. One of them had a bloody rag tied around his left thigh as a bandage. Three Horses smiled a little. Braddock had wounded one of the men trying to kill him.

Three Horses studied the pair for a long moment. They looked familiar, and when he was convinced they had been with Clete and Riggs and the other outlaws in Dinsmore that morning, he reached into his pocket and took out one of the long cartridges the Sharps used. These men were cold-blooded killers, and whatever happened to them, they had it coming.

He opened the breech and slid in the cartridge, then closed it and lifted the Sharps to his shoulder. It was heavy, and his hands and arms shook from the weight. He had to rest the barrel on a rock to steady the weapon.

Once he had done that, it was easier. He had a good view of both men, so he cocked the rifle and settled the sights on the one who wasn't wounded, figuring he was probably more of a threat because he was uninjured. When he was satisfied with his aim, Three Horses drew in a breath, held it, and squeezed the trigger.

The Sharps boomed and kicked back against his shoulder so hard it knocked him off his feet. He tumbled down the slope behind him, ass over teakettle, as the white men would say.

He had no idea whether or not the .50 caliber round had hit its target. All he could do was try to stop himself from falling and hope his head didn't hit a rock on the way down and bust wide open.

Chapter 9

When Braddock heard the buffalo gun go off, followed instantly by a shout that might have been pain or surprise or both, his instincts told him this was the only chance he would have to turn the tables on the bushwhackers. One of the rifles started to crack again, fast, as if the man using it was firing as fast as he could work the weapon's lever, and that made up Braddock's mind for him.

One of the bushwhackers was out of action, and the other was going after whoever was responsible for that.

Braddock leaped to his feet and raced toward the rocks, zigzagging a little to make himself a more difficult target as his boots pounded the hard ground.

As far as he could tell, nobody shot at him. He had the Winchester held at a slant across his chest with a round in the chamber, ready to go. As he reached the rocks, he darted between two of the big stone slabs and looked around, instantly spotting a man lying on his back with a bloody, fist-sized hole in his chest.

Not much doubt about where the bullet from that buffalo gun had gone, or that the man it had struck was dead.

Shots came from Braddock's right. He looked in that direction, saw a man standing there firing a rifle down the slope at something. The man's instincts must have alerted him to Braddock's presence, because he twisted around and tried to bring his rifle to bear on the Ranger.

Braddock's Winchester came up first and cracked as flame spurted from its muzzle. A puff of dust rose from the man's shirt as the bullet punched through the breast pocket and on into his chest. The slug's impact knocked the man back a step, and as he staggered, he lost his footing and fell backwards over the rim.

Braddock rushed over in time to see the man he had shot rolling down the slope. The loose-limbed way the man fell with his arms and legs flopping this way and that told Braddock he was dead.

Braddock didn't see anybody else, and he wondered what the bushwhacker had been shooting at back here—and who had killed the other man. Then he heard a weak voice call, "Ranger!" and spotted movement behind one of the stunted bushes that grew here and there on the escarpment's face.

The old Indian, Three Horses, pulled himself into view and struggled to stand. He propped himself up with an old Sharps carbine, holding on to the barrel with both hands as he rested the stock on the ground. Braddock hoped that antique wasn't loaded now, although he had a pretty good hunch Three Horses had used it to blow that hole in the first bushwhacker.

"Three Horses, what in blazes are you doing here?" Braddock asked.

The Indian grunted and said, "Saving your white hide, Ranger. I could use...a little help."

The old man was breathing hard, but as far as Braddock could see, he was only winded, not wounded. There were no blood stains on the ragged work clothes.

Braddock moved down the slope, sliding a little in places, and reached Three Horses' side. He grasped the old-timer's upper right arm and steadied him. They began to climb, with Three Horses holding the Sharps barrel in his left hand and using the carbine like a walking stick.

"I reckon that buffalo gun's what I heard go off a few minutes ago," Braddock said.

"Did I hit the man?"

"You blew a big hole right through one of them. And I killed the other one."

"We make a good team," Three Horses said.

Braddock wanted to tell the old Indian they weren't any kind of a team, good or otherwise, but he also knew that Three Horses had helped him out quite a bit. It would be a stretch to say that Three Horses had saved his life, because Braddock thought he could have held out until nightfall and dealt with the outlaws then, but this way he wouldn't have to waste the rest of the day holed up in those rocks. He could go ahead and get after Fenner and the others.

They had reached the top. Braddock still held Three Horses' arm as he nodded toward the dead man and asked, "Did you get a look at them? Were they part of the same bunch that raided Dinsmore?"

"I am certain of it," Three Horses said.

"Then we just whittled them down by twenty-five per cent."

"Yes. The odds against us are better now, although we are still outnumbered."

Braddock shook his head and said, "Not us. I don't know how you got here, but you're turning around and going back to Dinsmore."

"My honor is still not satisfied," Three Horses said as he lifted his chin defiantly.

"This isn't about honor. It's about the law. Bringing those men to justice is my job."

"Is it?"

Braddock stiffened. There was no way Three Horses could know that officially he wasn't a Texas Ranger anymore. The old-timer seemed to be pretty canny, though, despite his reputation back in town as a drunkard.

"Look, this is too dangerous for somebody your age—"

"I was not the one who was pinned down," Three Horses said as he looked coolly at Braddock.

"I would have gotten out of that spot."

"Perhaps."

"No maybe about it," Braddock snapped. "Do you have a horse?"

Three Horses hesitated, then said, "A mule."

"Go get it, and head back to Dinsmore."

"I will not."

"Then, damn it, if I have to arrest you—"

"Will you take me back yourself and lock me up?" Three Horses smiled. "If you do, the rest of those men will get away from you. You know that."

The worst part about it was that Braddock *did* know that.

Three Horses had given him a gift, and he was wasting it by standing around here jawing.

"All right," he said. "I guess I can't stop you from going wherever you want to. But I'll be damned if I'm going to wait around for you. You can keep up or not. And if there's more shooting, I won't be looking out for you, either. You'll be on your own and have to keep yourself alive."

"I am not worried. I am the—"

"The last war chief of the Comanches, I know," Braddock said.

He left the rocks and started to walk quickly toward his dun, which was still grazing in the distance. This ambush had already slowed him down enough.

Somewhere up ahead, Clete Fenner and five more outlaws were still on the loose, and heaven help anybody whose path happened to cross theirs.

Chapter 10

Dave Metcalf never got tired of looking at his wife Sheila. His favorite way to look at her, of course, was when she was undressed, like when she was rising out of the big galvanized bathtub with her creamy skin wet and gleaming, or gazing up at her when she was riding him, leaning forward slightly with an intent look on her face and her lower lip caught between her teeth and her thick blond hair hanging down, tickling his chest.

At moments like that, his first thought was about how much he loved her, and his second was to wonder how in the world a hardscrabble rancher who admittedly wasn't much to look at had ever talked a gorgeous woman like her into marrying him.

But he liked to look at her when she had her clothes on, too, like now when she came in with the apron she wore over a blue dress lifted and gathered to make a basket for the potatoes and beans and squash she had just gathered from their garden. Through the open door behind her, Dave could see the barn where his two hands, Luis and Clint, were leading in their horses after the day's work.

Dave had been out on the range with them earlier, but he had come on in to the house to finish up a letter he was writing so he could take it to Dinsmore and mail it the next day. He was buying some cattle from a rancher over by Callesburg, and the letter would finalize the deal.

Also, he had hoped that maybe he and Sheila could go in the bedroom for a spell, but she'd been too busy with her own chores, she said, and swatted him away...but with a smile that promised maybe next time it would be different.

"Gonna put those vegetables in the stew?" Dave asked his wife as she walked over to the stove where a big iron pot of water was already simmering.

"That's right. Did you finish what you were doing?"

"Got it right here," Dave said as he put his hand on the letter that sat on the rolltop desk in front of him. That desk had belonged to his late father, who'd been a professor of natural history at one of the universities back east. Dave hadn't followed him into teaching. He preferred being out living in nature, rather than lecturing about it in some stuffy old building.

He was glad he still had the desk to remind him of his father, though, who had been a kindly man at heart. Hauling it all the way out here by wagon hadn't been easy.

Dave stood up and moved toward Sheila, coming up behind her at the stove. Without looking around, she said, "Don't you go getting any ideas in your head. I'm busy, and Luis and Clint will be coming in here in just a few minutes."

"I can't help getting ideas," Dave said. "I just can't do anything about—"

A shot blasted somewhere outside.

The sound made both Dave and Sheila jump a little. Sheila's blue eyes were wide as she looked around and said, "What in the world?"

"One of the boys probably killed a snake," Dave said. "You know how many rattlers there are around here."

A little shudder went through Sheila at the reminder. She said, "I know. I always watch for them."

"I'll go see what happened," Dave said as he started toward the door. He glanced at the rifle and the shotgun hanging on hooks on the other side of the room but decided he wouldn't need either of them. Both of his riders carried belt guns for killing snakes.

He had just stepped through the door when somebody yelled and a gun went off again, then twice more, fast. A scream came from the barn. It sounded like Luis, Dave thought as fear suddenly burst inside him.

"Dave, what—" Sheila exclaimed as he whirled and lunged back into the house toward the weapons. Before he could get there, somebody kicked the back door open and a man rushed in and leveled a revolver at him. Dave skidded to a halt, terribly sure that he was about to die in the next heartbeat.

The man with the gun didn't pull the trigger, though. He just grinned at Dave and said, "Hold it right there, friend. No need for anybody else to get hurt." His eyes flicked toward Sheila for a second, and his grin widened as he looked back at Dave. "Your wife?"

"Y-yes," he forced out. "Please, don't shoot. Whatever you want, food, horses, whatever, just take it and leave." He thought about those cattle he'd been planning to buy and went on, "We...we even have some money saved up..."

"Well, ain't that enterprisin' of you. Don't worry, friend. We'll take it." The intruder looked at Sheila again and added, "We'll take it all."

Despair welled up inside Dave. He knew his pleas meant nothing, and so did the man's promise not to hurt them. The man wasn't alone. There were others out in the barn, and they had probably killed Luis and Clint by now. They would kill him, too, and they would take what they wanted from Sheila, all of them more than likely, before they killed her and burned the place to the ground. In that instant, Dave saw it all happen inside his head in horrifying detail, the unfolding images so terrible and ugly that he wanted to look away but couldn't.

So if he was doomed anyway, he might as well die fighting, he realized, and if there was even the slightest, tiniest chance that he and Sheila could survive...

All that flashed through his brain in the blink of an eye, and then his muscles tensed for a desperate leap. Before he could move, a step sounded behind him and something crashed against the back of his head.

The blow was enough to knock him to his knees. He felt like his brain was exploding inside his skull. He fell forward, twisting as he collapsed, and it seemed to take forever for him to land on his side on the rough plank floor.

As he did, he saw a man looming over him, gun in hand, and knew he'd been pistol-whipped from behind. The man was tall, broad-shouldered, with an angular, lantern-jawed face under his hat and not even a single ounce of mercy in his cold gray eyes.

Sheila screamed and bolted toward Dave. The man who had come in the back door hurriedly jammed his gun back in its holster and caught her, pulling her away as he wrapped his arms around her, pinning them to her sides. She kicked at him, but he swung her off the floor so that her struggles were futile.

"This fella was getting ready to jump you, Riggs," the second man said. "You were too busy looking at the woman to notice, weren't you? You're lucky I came in when I did."

"Ah, hell, Clete, you worry too much. I had the drop on him. If he'd come at me, I'd have shot him. It's better this way, though. He ain't dead, is he?"

Dave barely felt it as a boot toe prodded his side, but it was enough to make him moan.

"He's alive."

"Good. That way he can watch what we do to his pretty little wife. That'll be a show, won't it?"

"Later," Clete said. "After she's fixed some supper for us. I don't know about you, but I'm hungry."

"Yeah," Riggs said as he buried his face in Sheila's hair and laughed. "I'm damn near starvin'."

Chapter 11

A thin thread of smoke, almost invisible against the fading light in the sky, was the first indication something was ahead of them. Braddock had pulled the dun back to a walk to rest the horse when he spotted the smoke. He turned his head to look over his shoulder at Three Horses, who was about twenty feet behind him on the mule.

"I see it, too," the Indian said, somehow knowing what Braddock had been about to point out. "I saw it before you did, Ranger."

"Fine," Braddock said. "It doesn't matter who saw it first. Do you know where it's coming from?"

Three Horses said, "There are ranches up here. The people who live on them come into Dinsmore sometimes. But I do not know their names. They never had anything to do with me, except to look at me with pity or disgust as they passed on the street."

Braddock grunted. The old-timer sure liked to wallow in his misery. But he didn't have the right to make any judgments, Braddock told himself. He had done some wallowing, too, back in the days after Captain Hughes had told him he wasn't a Ranger anymore. Before he'd decided that it didn't matter what anybody else said: he would always be a Ranger.

Braddock stopped and waited for Three Horses to catch up to him. He said, "That's chimney smoke. Got to be from a ranch house. Fenner and his bunch likely saw it, too."

"Perhaps they went around, to avoid being spotted."

"Maybe...but it's more likely they stopped to loot the place."

And kill whoever lives there, Braddock added to himself.

Three Horses seemed to be thinking the same thing. He said, "The rancher and his family are in danger."

"Yeah. If they're still alive. But if they are, and we go busting in there without knowing the situation, it's liable to just make things worse for them."

"You need a scout," Three Horses said.

"I need to have a look-see for myself. You're going to stay here."

"You agreed to let me help."

"I did no such thing," Braddock said. "I told you I couldn't stop you from riding wherever you wanted to. But now I'm going to. You go stumbling around that bunch, you'll ruin everything."

Three Horses drew himself up straight in the saddle and gave Braddock a haughty look. He said stubbornly, "I will ride with you until we see what there is to see. Then...maybe I will wait."

That was probably the only concession he would get, thought Braddock. The old-timer's treatment at the hands of the outlaws had stung his pride so badly that he was determined to get his revenge, no matter what the cost. Braddock couldn't let that interfere with his job, but he supposed he could let it slide for the moment.

When the time came, he could tie and gag the old man if he had to, to make him stay put.

They rode on. The sun had just dipped below the horizon when they came in sight of several buildings sticking up from the plains. Braddock reined in and dismounted, motioning for Three Horses to do likewise. Out here on this flat land, the taller you were, the more visible you were.

Braddock had a pair of field glasses in his saddlebags. There was still enough light in the sky for him to see as he peered through the lenses.

The barn was the only structure built of planks, since lumber was at a premium out here on these mostly treeless plains. The main house and smaller bunkhouse were built of sod or adobe, Braddock couldn't tell which at this distance. He could see there were more than half a dozen horses in the corral next to the barn, though. That was a bad sign. The animals might not belong to Fenner and his gang, but chances were they did.

Three Horses tapped him on the shoulder. Braddock lowered the glasses and said, "What?"

The Indian pointed into the sky to the right of the barn. Braddock's eyes narrowed as he saw the dark shapes circling there, riding the gentle wind currents. He lifted the glasses again and squinted through them.

"There's something out there," he said a moment later. "Hard to tell for sure. It might be a couple of bodies, though."

"The carrion eaters will descend soon. They know death when they see it."

"Yeah." Braddock tracked the glasses back to the barn. Movement caught his eye. Two men stood in the barn's open doorway, gesturing as they talked. He saw the tiny orange specks that were the glowing ends of the quirlies they smoked. The men were roughly dressed, unshaven. Braddock knew outlaws when he saw them.

"It's Fenner and his gang, all right," he said. "They've killed a couple of people already. They dragged the carcasses out away from the barn. There are two men still there in front of the barn, probably keeping an eye on things."

"So four in the house," Three Horses said.

"More than likely." Braddock stowed the field glasses. "I need to get around behind the place and approach it from that angle. If I ride in from this way, they'll see me coming for sure." He looked at his companion. "You have to give me your word that you'll stay here."

Three Horses got that stubborn look on his wrinkled face again.

"They attacked the honor of a Comanche war chief," he said as if that explained everything.

"Damn it, Pete, if you don't give me your word, I'll—"

He didn't have to finish the threat. The old-timer raised his hand to stop him, sighed, and said, "Very well. You have my word. I will stay here and not interfere."

That was almost too easy, Braddock thought as he frowned. Maybe he ought to make sure and tie up the old fella anyway.

On the other hand, if he wound up dying this evening, Three Horses would be stuck here, tied up and unable to get away. He might be able to work himself loose eventually, but what if he wasn't? What if a rattlesnake came crawling along while the old-timer couldn't do anything about it?

And if the outlaws killed him, thought Braddock, there was a good chance they would look around to see if anyone else was in the area. They might find the Indian, and then Lord knew what they would do to him...

"All right, blast it. I'm going to have to take you at your word. I hope I can count on it."

Three Horses just folded his arms across his chest and gazed serenely at the Ranger.

"I'll come back and get you once I've dealt with those varmints," Braddock promised. "And if I don't come back, you head for Dinsmore. You can bring Deputy Bell and a posse back out here and pick up the trail again." He added grimly, "And bury anybody who needs burying."

Without waiting for Three Horses to respond, Braddock moved off to the east on foot, leading the dun. It was less likely the outlaws would spot him if he came in from that direction, rather than skylighting himself against the remaining light in the west. The edge of the Caprock was at least a mile away now, so he had plenty of room to do that.

As he moved into position, he wondered if Fenner and the others were getting curious about the two men they had left behind. Maybe, maybe not. They might not expect those two to rejoin them until later in the night or even in the morning. With their back trail covered like that, they might not be expecting trouble. Braddock hoped that was the case and that they wouldn't be quite as alert as a result.

With six-to-one odds, he would take any slight advantage he could get.

It took him about twenty minutes to get around the ranch headquarters and reach a spot half a mile north of the buildings. He left the dun there and started toward the place on foot, carrying the rifle and moving in a low crouch. He figured the outlaws wouldn't be expecting any trouble from this direction, but it never hurt to be careful.

Or rather, it *seldom* hurt to be careful, Braddock mused.

Sometimes a man just had to take a wild-ass chance.

Chapter 12

Braddock crawled the last couple of hundred yards, using the scrub brush for cover. This was the time of day rattlesnakes came out, but luck was with him and he encountered only a couple of the creatures. The snakes didn't coil up either time, but slithered off in disdain instead.

As far as he could see, Fenner hadn't posted any guards in back of the house. Braddock was able to crawl to within a few yards of the structure, which he could tell now was made from thick blocks of adobe. The back door was closed, but windows were on either side of it. He came up on one knee, then onto his feet and stole forward.

Glass panes were set in both windows. That probably cost the rancher quite a bit, but it made the place look nicer. Curtains hung on the inside of the glass, but they were pushed aside so that Braddock could see through. He checked the one to the left of the door first. It opened into a bedroom that was empty at the moment. Braddock could see the big four-poster bed in the dim light. The door to the rest of the house was closed.

He slid along the rear wall, past the door, and took off his hat as he edged his eye past the side of the other window.

This one gave him a view of the ranch house's large main room, which included both the kitchen and a living area. The place was furnished in what appeared to be functional but comfortable fashion, with a good-sized table that had four ladderback chairs around it, a fireplace with a couple of rocking chairs near it, and a rolltop desk with another ladderback chair. Woven rugs were scattered on the plank floor.

A dark-haired man lay on his side on one of those rugs in an awkward position because his arms were pulled behind his back and his wrists were lashed together. His ankles were bound as well. He was conscious but seemed groggy, as if he didn't quite know what was going on around him.

Braddock knew, though. He saw the four men sitting at the table with bowls of what looked like stew in front of them. They had torn hunks off a loaf of fresh bread, too, and were eating hungrily. Braddock recognized Clete Fenner right away from wanted posters he had seen. The others looked familiar as well, so he was sure their faces had decorated plenty of reward dodgers.

A very attractive blond woman stood beside the table. She wore a blue dress and a white apron, both of which were somewhat disheveled as if the men had been pawing her. Braddock didn't doubt that was what happened. She looked scared, as she had every right to be, but she looked angry, too.

The woman started to move away from the table, but the man closest to her reached out and closed his hand around her wrist.

"You know better than that, honey," he told her. Braddock had no trouble understanding the words because the window was raised a few inches to let fresh air into the room. "You need to stay right here close in case one of us needs anything. You don't wanna be rude to your guests, now do you?"

Fenner looked up with an expression of mild interest on his lean face. He asked, "What were you about to do, Mrs. Metcalf?"

The blonde said, "I have a pie over there in the keeper. I thought you might want some of it."

"Sounds good," Fenner said. "Riggs, go with her. Make sure she's not trying any sort of trick."

"No trick," the woman said. "It's just peach pie."

The outlaw called Riggs grinned and said, "That does sound mighty good. Let's you and me get it, honey. That'll just whet my appetite for more sweetness with you later on."

Braddock recalled that Riggs was one of the men who'd struck Three Horses back in Dinsmore, just before the gang hit the bank. The woman didn't respond to the veiled threat in the outlaw's voice. With Riggs beside her, she crossed the room to a pie keeper that sat on a shelf and opened it to take out the peach pie.

For a second, Braddock thought she was about to ram the pie tin into Riggs' face, and he was ready to move if she did so. He would have no choice but to kick the back door open, go in shooting, and hope for the best.

But then the fury he had seen on the woman's face disappeared as she regained control of her emotions, and she turned placidly back to the table, holding the pie in both hands. Riggs didn't seem to have noticed what had almost happened.

Outside the window, Braddock relaxed slightly. He wouldn't have to make his move just yet, although he knew that his time was running out fast.

What he needed was some sort of distraction, something that would draw the four killers out of the house. Then he could go in fast while the woman escaped out the back, and take them from behind. With any luck he could drop a couple of them before they knew what was going on, and then he would take his chances with the others.

He was still trying to figure out what that distraction might be when one of the men from the barn appeared in the open front door and said, "Clete, you got to see this."

Fenner looked up and asked, "What is it? Are Chuck and Gardner here already?"

Chuck and Gardner—those would be the two men who'd ambushed him, thought Braddock.

The man at the door shook his head and said, "No, but it's something I've never seen before."

Mrs. Metcalf set the pie on the table as Fenner stood up impatiently. As he started toward the door, he said, "All right, but this better be worth it, Gant."

"Oh, it is," Gant said.

Curious, the other men stood up and started to follow Fenner. The boss outlaw glanced back and snapped, "Riggs, you stay here and keep an eye on the woman and her husband."

"Ah, hell, Clete—" Riggs began.

"Just do it."

Riggs shrugged and smiled at the blonde, saying, "I don't care what's out there anyway. I'd rather spend my time with you, darlin'." He ran a hand up her arm and slid his fingers along the line of her jaw before cupping her chin.

Braddock ducked down to move below the window as he eased over to the rear corner of the ranch house. He was just as curious as the others about what the man called Gant had spotted. He wasn't expecting what he saw.

Sitting out there on the back of his mule a hundred yards away, dressed in full Comanche regalia, including beaded buckskins and a tall, feathered headdress, was Three Horses. He held the Sharps carbine with the stock propped against his right thigh so the barrel pointed at the sky. With the light behind him, he was a pretty impressive figure. He would have been more impressive on a Comanche pony instead of a mule, but a fella had to work with what he had available.

The five outlaws were at the edge of Braddock's view, partially concealed by the building as they stood there staring at Three Horses. A couple of them laughed, but one man said with a nervous edge in his voice, "I didn't think there were any savage Indians still around, Clete. I thought they were all up in Oklahoma these days."

"That's not a savage Indian," Fenner said disdainfully. "That's just a crazy old man. In fact...Riggs, come out here. I think that old redskin from Dinsmore must have followed us."

Braddock whirled back to the window. He had wanted a distraction, and Three Horses, despite breaking his word, had given him one. If Riggs would just leave the woman inside, Braddock could get in there, free her and her husband, and then hell could go ahead and start to pop.

Riggs wasn't going to leave the woman, though. He grasped her upper left arm to drag her along with him as he said, "Come on, honey. Killin' an old Injun ought to be some good sport. Get me nice and worked up for you later on."

They had taken a couple of steps when the blonde reached under her apron with her free hand, brought out a small pistol from somewhere, and jammed the barrel against the side of Riggs' head as she pulled the trigger. The gun went off with a little pop, not loud at all, and Riggs staggered. Braddock knew a small caliber slug like that would bounce around inside a man's skull and turn his brain into mush.

Around on the other side of the cabin, Three Horses kicked the mule into a run, let out a high-pitched whoop, and charged through the dusk.

Chapter 13

Since Braddock was closer to the door than the corner, he booted it open and ran inside. Riggs had collapsed to leak blood onto the floor from the bullet hole in his head, but Mrs. Metcalf was on her feet and swung the little revolver in her hand toward the stranger who had just burst into her house.

"Texas Ranger!" Braddock called out so she wouldn't shoot him, too. "Stay with your husband and stay down!"

He reached the doorway in time to see the other five outlaws starting to scatter as startled exclamations came from them. They clawed out their revolvers, but Three Horses was still out of range of the handguns.

The outlaws weren't out of range of the Sharps, though. Somehow the old-timer found the strength to fire it on the run, its heavy boom rolling through the twilight. Braddock knew the shot wasn't going to hit anything—

That thought had just gone through his brain when an outlaw's head flew apart like a dropped pumpkin. Lucky shot or not, the man was just as dead either way.

With everything that was going on, the remaining desperadoes hadn't noticed Braddock yet. Normally he would have called on them in the name of the State of Texas, ordering them to drop their guns, elevate, and surrender.

But with all the blood these men had on their hands, he didn't hesitate to bring the Winchester to his shoulder and open fire.

Sharp cracks split the air as he drilled two of the outlaws and sent them spinning off their feet. Fenner and the remaining man were triggering at the still charging Three Horses, who continued to whoop madly as he galloped toward them.

Three Horses was in range now, and he jerked back as lead found him. He couldn't stay on the mule. He slid sideways and then pitched off.

Braddock planted a slug between the shoulder blades of the fifth man, knocking him forward onto his face, where he landed in a limp sprawl.

That left Fenner, and he moved with the speed that had kept him alive for this long in his perilous career as a badman. He whirled toward Braddock and got a shot off, coming close enough that Braddock felt the heat of the bullet as it whipped past his ear.

Then Braddock slammed three rounds into Fenner's chest as fast as he could work the Winchester's lever and the outlaw went over backward. With his arms outflung, he writhed in the dust for a second, arching his back, then died with one leg drawn up and the knee cocked at the sky, where stars were beginning to appear against the deep blue in the east.

Braddock levered another cartridge into the Winchester's chamber, just in case, then slowly lowered the rifle. He looked at the bodies scattered all around.

"Are...are they all dead?" Mrs. Metcalf asked from the door behind him.

"I'm pretty sure they are," Braddock replied. "But pretty sure isn't good enough."

He went from body to body, making certain that they were, indeed, corpses. He was tempted to put a few more bullets in them, just for good measure, but he figured he would have enjoyed that too much. He looked at Mrs. Metcalf and nodded instead, to let her know she was safe now.

She looked at the pistol in her hand and said, "I carry it for snakes."

"I'd say that's how you used it," Braddock said.

"I'm surprised none of them found it while they were pawing me. I guess they were too careless. Or they weren't meant to find it."

Things like that were beyond Braddock's reckoning. He told the woman, "Stay here and take care of your husband," then started walking toward the fallen figure of Three Horses.

By the time he got there, he was running.

He slid to a stop, dropped to one knee, and rolled the old

Indian onto his back. There was a dark stain on the buckskin shirt, high on the right side.

Three Horses grunted and said, "Be careful. I've been shot."

"I can see that," Braddock said, surprisingly grateful to find that the old man was alive. "You gave me your word you'd stay out of this."

"Old Pete gave you his word. Three Horses, the last war chief of the Comanche, did not." He sighed. "Are our enemies all dead?"

"Every last one of them."

"This is good. The honor of the Comanche people has been avenged, at least this one last time." Another sigh came from the old man. "I see stars above me. They welcome me to the realm of the spirits. It is a good day to die."

Three Horses' eyes closed.

"Die, hell," Braddock said. "Unless all your blood's dried up so that you don't have any to spare, you'll be fine. Looks like that bullet went straight through without doing much damage."

Three Horses opened one eye and said, "Really?"

"Really," Braddock told him. "Let's get you on your feet. If you can walk to that ranch house, there's a lady there who I'll bet can patch you up. She's got some peach pie, too."

"Peach pie," Three Horses repeated.

"I thought that might get you moving," Braddock said.

He helped the old man to his feet, carried the rifle in his left hand, and put his left arm around Three Horses' waist to support him as they walked slowly toward the ranch house where both of the Metcalfs waited now.

"You had all this get-up in that carpetbag you carry around, didn't you?"

"This get-up, as you call it, is the way a Comanche war chief should dress."

"Maybe so. I'll admit, it looks all right on you."

"Is there...a reward...for those men?"

"Sure. I expect it'll add up to quite a bit. If I was you, I'd share it with these folks. They deserve something for what they've gone through, and anyway, it was the lady who killed Riggs."

Three Horses sighed and said, "I would have liked to kill him myself. But I am glad he is dead. He had it coming."

"No argument from me," Braddock said.

After a moment, the old man asked, "You are not going to stay and claim any of the reward?"

"No, now that it's all over and justice has been done, I have to move on."

"Of course. The hole in your badge. Some things appear true and are false. Some things appear false and are true."

"You talking about the two of us or just spouting philosophy like a dime novel Indian?"

Instead of answering, Three Horses asked, "Have you ever thought about having someone to ride along with you on your journeys?"

"Like Natty Bumppo and Chingachgook, you mean?"

Three Horses snorted and said, "Someone has to get you out of trouble, white man."

Braddock shook his head and said, "That's not happening in a million years," as they limped on slowly through the dusk.

About the Author

James Reasoner has been a professional writer for nearly forty years. In that time, he has authored several hundred novels and short stories in numerous genres. Writing under his own name and various pseudonyms, his novels have garnered praise from Publishers Weekly, Booklist, and the Los Angeles Times, as well as appearing on the New York Times, USA Today, and Publishers Weekly bestseller lists. He lives in a small town in Texas with his wife, award-winning fellow author Livia J. Washburn. His blog can be found at http://jamesreasoner.blogspot.com .

More great Westerns by James Reasoner!

OUTLAW RANGER

G.W. Braddock was raised to be a Texas Ranger and never wanted anything else. But when he's stripped of his badge through no fault of his own and a corrupt system turns the vicious killer Tull Coleman loose on the people of the Lone Star State, Braddock has to decide if he's going to follow the law—or carry out the job he was born to do, even if it means becoming an outlaw himself!

OUTLAW RANGER #2: HANGMAN'S KNOT

Hell came to Santa Angelina on a beautiful morning, as the Texas settlement was practically wiped out by vicious outlaws led by the bloodthirsty lunatic Henry Pollard. Now Pollard is in jail in Alpine, waiting on his trial and an all but certain date with the hangman. The only real question is whether an outraged lynch mob will string him up first. Not everyone wants to see Pollard dance at the end of a rope, however. His gang of hired killers would like to set him free, and so would his older brother, a wealthy cattleman who has always protected Pollard from the consequences of his savagery. Riding into the middle of this three-cornered war is the Outlaw Ranger, G.W. Braddock, who may not have a right anymore to wear the bullet-holed star-in-a-circle badge pinned to his shirt, but whose devotion to the law means he'll risk his life to see that justice is done!

OUTLAW RANGER #3: BLOOD AND GOLD

A savage ambush...twenty men slaughtered in a brutal massacre...a fortune in gold stolen! This was a crime big enough and bold enough to bring the Outlaw Ranger to the wide-open settlement of Cemetery Butte, where a powerful mining tycoon rode roughshod over any who dared to oppose him. But even that atrocity doesn't prepare G.W. Braddock for the evil that awaits him, stretching bloody hands out of the past. Gritty, compelling, and packed with action, the saga of the Outlaw Ranger continues in BLOOD AND GOLD, the third exciting installment in this series from bestselling author James Reasoner.

LONE STAR FURY

A plea for help from a woman he thought was dead brings Texas Ranger Jim Hatfield to the ghost town of Palminter. What he finds waiting for him is a storm of outlaw bullets—and an even deeper mystery that leads him to a mansion on top of a sinister mesa overlooking the Rio Grande. To survive, the legendary Lone Wolf will need his keen wits—and all his deadly gun skill!

LAST CHANCE CANYON

Only desperate men dared to venture into Last Chance Canyon, like bounty hunter Rye Callahan and the deadly outlaw he pursued. The fate that awaited them inside the lonely box canyon was something neither man could have anticipated, and the question was whether either of them would make it out alive!

LAST STAGECOACH TO HELL!

Bounty hunter Rye Callahan risked his life to capture the brutal outlaw Ike Blaine in a desert showdown. But an even deadlier danger awaits both men when they board the stagecoach bound for an isolated Arizona settlement with a sinister secret. Callahan will need all his cunning and gun skill to survive this trip on the last stagecoach to Hell!

Made in the USA
Lexington, KY
26 April 2016